VAMPIRE

CRUSADER

The Immortal Knight Chronicles
Book 1

Richard of Ashbury
and the Third Crusade
June 1190 to November 1192

DAN DAVIS

Vampire Crusader

Copyright © 2015 by Dan Davis

For information contact:

dandaviswrites@outlook.com

ISBN: 9781520978710

First Edition: April 2017

For B.B. Dade.

Author, historian, sick man

CHAPTER ONE
THE OATH

RIDERS GALLOPED AWAY from Ashbury manor house at dawn. I had slept in the wood again. The shadows were long but the first rays of the morning sun warmed my face as I walked to the house.

Though I was tired, I hurried. My brother's crossbow had to be returned before he woke, as I had promised never to touch it again.

It is impossible to sleep late when you sleep outside. You wake to the din of birdsong and light. Yet waking early has its rewards. The thought of fresh bread, hot from the ovens, made my mouth water.

But then hooves drummed against the earth and men

jeered from beyond the hedgerows. The clamour shattered the morning and startled a pair of crows into flight overhead, cawing in protest.

I knew the sound of men with their blood up when I heard it. I ran forward, crashing through the mature barley.

The manor house was not a popular place. Visitors were rare, especially since my brother had turned even more sullen than he used to be. He had a handful of friends but none of those dour knights and lords would holler and whoop in such a way. Not at sunrise. Not for any reason.

My sword and mail I had stashed in a chest back at my woodland camp. The crossbow in my hands was useless because Martha had lost the last of the bolts in the undergrowth.

I tossed it and ran on. The only weapon I had was my dagger.

From the noise of the hooves and whinnying and the cries of the men, I guessed there were five or ten of them galloping off. By the time I pushed through the hedge onto the road they were almost away.

The last rider glanced back as he disappeared beyond the hill on the wooded road to Lichfield. He was a knight dressed in mail with a shield slung across his back. His surcoat was red. I could make out no further detail and yet something about him was familiar.

But he was in shadow and then he was gone.

I ran to the boundary of the manor house and leapt the drystone wall and ditch.

My brother's horses whinnied from the stables on the other side of the house. None of the dogs barked.

The hall door was open. A splintered hole had been hacked through the centre. The doorway was a black void.

I threw myself into the great hall.

The stench of warm blood and torn bowels was overwhelming. I retched.

The mutilated bodies of the servants lay all over. The old, the young, the men and the women had all been dragged into the hall and slaughtered.

I knelt by a few, hoping that some would yet live. Most were still warm to the touch but their wounds were terrible. Throats gouged out. Bellies slit open. Daggers punched through the eyes. There were no survivors.

The fire was unlit and the windows shuttered so I could not see clearly but none of the dead appeared to be my brother, his wife or their children.

A noise. From the floor above. No more than a faint scraping upon the boards.

I gripped my dagger and ran through the great hall through to the rooms beyond, crying out for Henry and for Isabella.

There were more bodies lying in the passage to the pantry and buttery but I went the other way, into the parlour. Streaks of blood led through the door out to the stable and more stained the stairway up to the solar. I leapt up the stairs, ran through the solar and barged through the open door to their bedchamber.

I froze.

"Isabella," I cried.

She lay on her back by the bed in a pool of blood. It soaked her dress and her eyes had rolled up, the lids half closed. A jagged gash had ripped through one shoulder and half her neck was in tatters. The splintered edge of her collarbone jutted from the wet, sucking wound.

I knelt in her blood and lifted the back of her head with one hand. Only the fact that blood flowed and bubbled from the lacerations suggested she had not yet died. But there was no chance that she would live.

"Henry?" Isabella mumbled, her eyes flickering open.

"It is Richard." I clutched her hand in mine. Her skin as cold and white as marble.

"Richard." Her voice a whisper. Her eyes unfocused.

"What happened? Who were those men?"

Her eyes stared through me, unseeing. Or perhaps she saw Death.

Blood had been flung about the room; sprays of it

reaching the painted ceiling above us. I could taste it in the air. Yet there was no other body.

"Where is Henry, my lady? Where is your husband?"

"Gone," she whispered. "Slain."

"The children?" I said, though I did not want to ask.

She squeezed her eyes shut. "He killed them." She sobbed and blood streamed from her mouth. "Oh God, he killed my babies."

I struggled for breath. "Who?"

"Satan himself." There was blood in her voice and she coughed, struggling for breath.

Perhaps I should have told her that she would soon see her sweet children in Heaven.

I could have told her that I loved her, that I would do anything for her. But in that moment the weeks and months of my romantic infatuation were insignificant. Absurd, even.

I should certainly have told her to lay still and held her as she drew her last breath.

Instead of compassion, I was full of outrage and wrath.

All I wanted was to destroy.

"Who do you name as Satan?" I demanded, lifting her head up further. "Isabella. Who were those men?"

Her head rolled back and I grasped it and held it up to mine.

My voice rose. "Isabella."

Her eyes flickered open and she breathed, shuddering then coughed a spray of blood.

"Richard?" Her voice was weak, confused. She had always been so slight, so delicate but she clung on to the last moments of her life.

"I am here." I squeezed her cold hand, blinking away tears.

"Richard." Her voice was so quiet I stilled my breath to hear it. "Richard, it was William." She coughed more blood, fighting for breath.

I struggled to understand. I had assumed that war had come to Derbyshire. That the Welsh had attacked across the border or the Scots had somehow raided this far south.

"William? Earl William de Ferrers did this?"

I should not have been quite so surprised.

"Richard," she said, grasping my arm with desperate strength. She opened her beautiful eyes wide to look deep into mine. "Richard, you must avenge your brother's death. Avenge the death of his children."

"I will, my lady."

"Swear it."

"I shall not rest, I shall not live, I shall not die until William lies dead by my sword. This I swear to you and to Almighty God with all my heart."

Her mouth twitched. "Amen."

She died. Her last breath a sigh that was stoppered with blood. I held her as she choked and drowned on what little blood remained in her body.

It was 1190. In the eight hundred years since that day, I have travelled the world in pursuit of my enemy, William de Ferrers. Many times, over many centuries and in many lands I fought him.

William left a trail of horror in his wake. I did my duty to avenge all those that he and his followers slaughtered. I spent centuries hunting and destroying the monsters that he made. Always he made more.

Wherever there was great death and evil in the world, William was never far. I fought him in the New World, the Far East and in Napoleon's Europe. I tracked him through the horrors of the Black Death and the overwhelming destruction on the Eastern Front.

He was crusader, outlaw, khan. He was a count, a cavalier and a cardinal.

William was a murderer, a devil.

A vampire.

My brother Henry lay eviscerated, beheaded and

dismembered in the courtyard between house and stables. I gathered the pieces of his body together.

His strong face, in life so often twisted in anger, was now blank. One eyelid was open and full of blood. As though it was staring at me in silent accusation.

"I slept in the wood again, Henry," I told his head, holding it in my hands. "I only just missed them."

It was a scorching summer morning. Yellowhammers chirped and warbled in the trees above as I dug graves for my family. I lined them up next to the recent grave of our father and the much older grave of our mother.

The ground was baked hard but I was young and strong and hacked through into the softer soil beneath.

I laid Henry's limbs in the grave beside his torso. His guts I had pushed back in as much as I could. Luckily, I had not eaten for a day or so, otherwise I would certainly have vomited.

I stopped and eased off Henry's rings from his pale, stubby fingers. One was the signet ring that had belonged to our father. The ash tree emblem was worn almost flat. I ran my finger over it and I felt an echo of the anger that had flared up between my brother and me over that ring. I had argued that it should have been buried along with the old man. In truth, I had wanted it for myself. After all, Henry had inherited every other object, title and land. But Henry had flown into a blind rage at my suggestion and had remained sullen until I acquiesced. By then he had already taken to wearing it.

I scooped out a handful of dirt from my father's grave and pushed the ring into it.

I found few remains of the children. The baby Henry had been barely out of swaddling and Joanna was still often falling when she tried to run. There was not much of them to find.

I gathered those parts together in a blanket and wrapped them up into a bundle. I placed them in their grave together even though I was unsure whether such a thing was allowed. But those sweet children had been inseparable in life and I wanted them to share their resting place.

I knew I should summon the prior from Tutbury to speak the necessary prayers. But I was numb. And there was much work to do that day.

The servants I dragged into a single long grave along the edge of the consecrated area. I hoped they would not mind sharing their burial. I was sure to dig it north to south and laid the bodies side by side so that everyone would wake, on the day of judgement, facing the rising sun. Ashbury was a small estate by any standard but still we had two dozen servants and labourers to see to the house and to the land.

Many of the bodies had their throat and neck hacked

out, just as Isabella had suffered.

Almost all slain in such a manner were women.

I found Barbary, Isabella's wet nurse, strung up by her ankles from a beam in the kitchen. There were pails under her that had the residue of fresh blood coating the inside. A funnel, still dribbling blood, had been tossed into a corner. Barbary's skin was as white as chalk and she seemed to have been drained from slashes through her neck.

It reminded me of the time I had watched a pig slaughtered at Duffield Castle. The creature's blood was drained and saved for sausages and blood cakes. I watched that pig screaming and bucking as it died, flinging itself around in mindless terror.

Barbary must have gone the same way but there were also teeth marks gouged into her breasts and belly. I cut the poor woman down and covered her up with sacking before carrying her to the grave.

Most knights favoured the sword for its versatility and prestige. Others used mace or falchion or axe. I wondered what form of weapon the murderers had used to tear and shred the necks of my family and servants. Likely a dagger, worried back and forth. I was training to be a knight from the age of seven and we learned the quickest, simplest ways to kill a man. That the murderers had used such elaborate, unnecessary methods was alarming.

In the cellar were three more bodies in a heap. Their blood pooled along with the cider and ale leaking from barrels hacked open and thrown over. I kicked the rats away from the bodies and carried them one at a time up the long grave.

My mind was shattered. I'd never seen much death and blood and it seemed the horrors would never end. I felt the world turn under me, somehow. When I had awoken that morning, the world had been one way. Then, after I stepped through the door to the hall, everything had changed, forever.

The last of the bodies in the cellar was that of Mabel. She was a simple old woman with a twisted back who cleaned in the kitchen and scrubbed the floors. Her neck was slashed almost clean through. When I lifted the body the last vestiges of her decrepit skin ripped off and the head thudded to the floor and rolled over once.

Someone gasped and whimpered in the darkness.

I lay old Mabel's body down by her head, grabbed the lamp and explored behind the remaining barrels in the corner where the noise was coming from.

The girl hunched in the corner, her hands over her hair. She was the daughter of Osbert, the man who tended the gardens and brewed sour ale. I had already dragged his body to the grave.

"Rose," I said, my voice so loud and sudden that she jumped out of her skin. I tried again in a soft whisper. "Rose. It is Richard."

She kept up the whimpering to herself. The girl could manage no more than fragments of words. No amount of coaxing could elicit any further response so I scooped her up as gently as I could. She flinched but then clung to me. Rose was an ugly child, with prominent teeth and no chin. She had pissed herself and was shivering in a thin dress that stuck to her legs.

"The bad men have gone," I whispered as I held her to me. "No one can hurt you now."

She buried her face into my chest and I held it there as I stepped over Mabel's remains.

"Keep your eyes closed, child," I whispered.

Not all the servants were killed. Walt and Marge had hid in the orchard and when the killers had left they ran through the wood all the way to the priory for help.

I stepped out of the house carrying Rose and found Prior Theobald riding his pony toward the manor house with a group of brothers scurrying behind on foot.

They were almost up to the door and when they saw me they froze. The monks turned to the prior and the prior's face drained of what little colour it had.

I glanced down. There was blood all over me.

Poor Rose. Blood covered the girl, too, where I had carried her against my sodden clothes. I must have looked like a creature from a nightmare and still she had allowed me to carry her away from that cellar. To the prior we must have appeared as the risen dead.

"Help us," I cried.

Prior Theobald spurred into action and rode up. Even mounted he seemed small.

"By God, Richard," the old man's voice shook and his eyes betrayed the horror they saw. "What have you done?"

I did not understand at first so I merely stared in response.

But, thank God, he took control. He took control of me, of the girl and the surviving servants.

"Ride hard for the sheriff," the prior said to a young monk and handed over the reins of his pony. The prior kept his eyes on me.

"I did not do this thing," I mumbled. "There were riders on the road."

The prior looked disturbed. He nodded.

"For the love of God, someone take this child away from him," Prior Theobald said.

Our servant Marge came hurrying after the prior. She took Rose away toward the village. The girl seemed to be staring back at me from over Marge's shoulder. But her eyes looked through me, into the past. Into Hell itself.

"It is a miracle that the girl survived this," the prior said, reaching for something holy to say. "We should all be thankful for that small mercy."

I wanted to smash his teeth down his throat for uttering such nonsense. There was nothing to be thankful for. But the good prior was kind enough to have his monks and lay brothers help. They took over the burials while I sat in dumb shock upon the wall outside.

"You are the lord of Ashbury now, Richard," the prior said, perched next to me.

The new sheriff, Roger de Lacy arrived with his men in a thunder of hooves late that afternoon. He had me escorted to the Priory. His men even watched while I scrubbed the blood from myself and dressed in clothes the prior provided. The prior insisted I be allowed to wash before being questioned.

The Bishop of Coventry had been visiting the sheriff. He came along to Tutbury Priory to question me, too. The bishop was one of the most powerful men in the kingdom. Not merely a bishop, he was also Sheriff of Warwickshire, Leicestershire and Staffordshire.

It was dark when the sheriff and the bishop sat me down at Prior Theobald's sturdy table. It was one of the few private places in the priory. As I walked in, I heard the bishop arguing that I be taken to the nearest castle or anywhere that had a dungeon or with a sturdy door.

They were sitting to discover my guilt.

The bishop stared across the table with ill-concealed hostility. Bishop Hugh de Nonant was a big man, almost as tall as me and heavily muscled. I had always thought he looked like an ox herder rather than a man of God. But men so filled with ambition have little room in their souls for holiness. And the bishop was about as holy as a turnip.

The sheriff sat to my right, scratching words onto parchment every now and then while we spoke. The prior sat at my left side and said little but I welcomed his familiar presence. Before me was a jug of wine and while we sat I drank my way down the road toward oblivion.

"Where were you when this happened, Richard?" Roger de Lacy was not much older than I was. The sheriff had inherited vast estates across central England. He was Sheriff of Derbyshire and Nottinghamshire. I had come into my brother's blood-soaked manor.

"The sheriff asked you a question, boy," the bishop said, his voice a deep rumble. "Why do you claim you were not at home?"

I sighed and drank.

"Perhaps we should let the man sleep," the sheriff suggested. He was short but with big bones and a lumpy head. Scabbed pimples and a wispy beard covered his face. His eyes were soft and brown and seemed kind.

"He will speak first," the bishop said, overruling the sheriff. "Then he may rest."

"I was in the wood," I said, which was true. "Shooting Henry's crossbow."

"We are informed you often meet with a girl from the village," the sheriff said, glancing at the prior.

"Martha," the prior said quietly.

I nodded. How often our secrets turn out to be common knowledge.

I drank down my cup of wine. It roiled in my empty belly. My hands were shaking and the cup rattled on the table as I set it down.

"You have told us it was Earl William de Ferrers who did this... this evil thing. But did you see him do it, Richard? Did you see the murders happen? If so, how did you survive?"

"If your story is true," the bishop said. "It means you hid like a coward. And if you are lying, well..." He sneered at me. He was trying to scare me but I had looked through the gates of Hell that morning. Still, I had no desire to be executed.

"I saw the merest glimpse of a group of men galloping away," I said to the sheriff. "I did not see who they were."

"Ha." The bishop slapped the table with his meaty hand. "What did I tell you?"

The sheriff ignored him. "Then why say it was Earl William?"

He poured me more wine and I drank before answering. Chucking that dark, sour stuff into my stomach made me sick but I needed it.

"Isabella told me," I said. "Before she died."

"A likely story," the bishop said. "Very convenient, indeed."

"Convenient?" My voice rose and the bishop's jowls grew red. I bit back my anger. "Walt and Marge saw the murderers, surely? They came to tell you, prior. What did they see?"

Prior Theobald opened his mouth to answer but the bishop jabbed his finger at him.

"Say not a word," the bishop said. "This man may be a murderer. Until we decide he is not then he does not get to make demands of us."

I could not believe they could be so dense. "Why do you not ask Earl William where he and his monsters were last night instead of gathering about me? I swore to bring him to justice. If you lords will not provide it then, by God, I shall take it for myself."

"A shame you did not take justice this morning," the

bishop said, sneering.

I lurched to my feet, bumping into the table, my chair scraping upon the floor and intending to shout. But my voice cracked as I spoke. "I could not have known what they had done," I said.

The bishop held my gaze for but a moment before he looked away.

The sheriff stood too and placed a hand on my arm. "William has gone," the sheriff said. "It is certain that he rode out from Duffield Castle last night. He rode with his six knights, armoured as if for war, so the servants say. He has not returned."

I felt the anger leech out of me and I sat again. The sheriff poured more wine into my cup.

"He could have gone anywhere," the bishop said, sulking. "It proves nothing."

"You were a friend of Earl Robert," I said to the bishop. "You visited many times. You know what William is like."

The bishop pursed his lips for a moment. "I do not see what my friendship with the late Earl has to do with this. And I am surprised to hear you of all men speak ill of—"

"I admired Earl Robert," I said, hearing the wine in my voice. "I was ever grateful that he had taken me away from Ashbury."

In truth, he scared me from the first day until the day he

died. Robert was huge and stern and he beat me with his own hand. Which I suppose was an honour, of sorts.

"I know William," I said to the sheriff. "I knew him from when I was a child up until he went away to the Holy Land. And the first thing I learned at Duffield Castle was to stay away from William de Ferrers. My first night, in the hall, he coaxed over a cat using some meat. He stroked it. Then he speared it through the chest with a long dagger and tossed it still living into the fire. He did it just to frighten me, I think." I drank down my cup. My hands would not stop shaking.

"William killed a cat?" the bishop said and scoffed. "Good. Cats are evil. Anyway, boys have been the same since time out of mind."

"He must have been fifteen or sixteen and almost a man. Old enough to know better."

"And William went to the Holy Land years ago," the sheriff said. "And came back because his father was dying?" Despite owning so much land nearby, the sheriff did not yet know our shire.

"No," the bishop said, shaking his massive head.

"He was in fine health," I said. "He stuffed himself senseless with a whole mushroom pie in the evening and the next day he was dead."

"Never a heartier man in all Christendom." The bishop

nodded. "Strong as bull. But you can never trust a mushroom."

"That was when you returned to Ashbury," the sheriff said, scratching away on his parchment. "Your brother was lord by then."

"Me and the other lads were told to leave in the same breath William used to tell us Earl Robert was dead."

"What other lads got thrown out?" the bishop asked.

"Curzon, Baskerville, Levett," I said, tallying them on my fingers. "Vipont, Barduff. And the rest."

The bishop grunted. "Good families."

"What did you all do to warrant expulsion from William's service?" the sheriff asked.

"William brought his own knights back from the Holy Land. Proper fighters, he said, not whelps like us. He said he could not afford to keep us as well as them."

The bishop shrugged. "You boys were his father's men. Makes sense that a lord would want loyal followers."

"When I left he said that he would make everything up to me," I said, taking another drink.

They all exchanged a look that I was too tired to interpret.

"What did you think he meant by it?" the sheriff said.

"I was the strongest knight," I said. "I believed he intended to take me back into his service once the others were too far away to take it as a slight. I was wrong."

The bishop shifted his huge bulk forward to peer at me. "Perhaps it was you he was hoping to kill last night?"

I had not considered that. "If that were the case, what reason would he have for slaying every living soul in the house?"

"There is no reason here," the prior said, his throat dry and raspy with emotion. "Only madness. Madness and evil. Those men are devils, perhaps, or even Satan himself."

After a pause, the sheriff continued with his questions. "You returned to Ashbury and yet you sleep in the woods?"

I shifted in my seat and took a drink. "It is a fine summer," I said. "I made a camp down by the stream. I practice with sword and crossbow by day."

"And by night you practice with young Martha," the bishop said, smirking. The prior scowled at him which made the bishop laugh. "Tell me, son. Does her father know you are ruining his daughter?"

The bishop liked to take local girls into his service. Especially the poor ones with no family to protest when he started feeling them up. And worse.

"Martha is a decent girl," I said. "All she wants is to learn to shoot the crossbow." We kissed often and fumbled at each other through our clothing. But Martha was too bright to give up her virginity to me.

"Shooting your crossbow right up her, morning, noon and night, I wager." The bishop chuckled to himself.

The sheriff coughed. "A crossbow is hardly a knight's weapon."

"The crossbow intrigues me, is all. After his time in the Holy Land, Henry brought the weapon back from Aragon."

"Along with his wife," the bishop added and smirked as if he'd been clever.

"Forgive me," the sheriff said. "But I hear that you often quarrel with your brother?"

I understood that they believed William and I had committed the crime together. Or at least that I was involved in the massacre in some way.

Everyone had heard that I quarrel often with Henry.

I remembered my father's voice. *You take after your damned mother.* Before I had gone to Duffield Castle my father would often shout and batter me about the head. *You clumsy oaf. You useless goat turd. Why could you have not been like Henry?*

And then there was Isabella.

Isabella was far above his station. She had an astonishing, delicate beauty. She seemed utterly out of place in dusty old Ashbury manor but her family in Aragon had fallen upon hard times. It was enough of a disgrace that she was willing to stoop as low as a poor English knight.

Henry wanted me gone. Wanted me to offer my service to someone, anyone who would take me.

Go to the Holy Land, Richard. By God, there is nothing for you here.

He would fly into a rage at the smallest thing. The servants I was friendly with had told me he had become that way since I returned from Duffield. It was my presence that had made him so volatile.

I did not know what I had done to anger him so and had no desire to stay with him. But I could not bear the thought of being apart from Isabella. So I stayed in the wood all that summer, fretting on an inevitable future apart from her. And yet doing nothing.

"I had no quarrel with Henry," I said.

They looked at each other, knowing I was lying.

The bishop stared. "Yet your father had a falling out with your brother, many years ago, if I recall?"

My eyes ached. Their pointless questions and prying into my life was more than I could bear. And, after swallowing cup after cup of wine along with my anger, I was drunk and my guts were churning.

"William and his knights did this," I said to the bishop, the sheriff and the prior. "Those men. You know his men? If you knew them, my lords, you would not be asking me so many questions."

"Please name and describe them to me. My bailiffs must know exactly who they are looking for," the sheriff said, ready to write on his parchment. "William is dark of hair and tall, is that correct?"

"Tall as me, if not taller. But he is much older, close to thirty, I think."

"Thirty and unmarried?" the sheriff asked. "Are all his men unmarried? Are they perhaps sodomites?"

"How dare you," the bishop growled. "Robert's son is no sodomite. He has been at war with the heathens for many years, I am sure he will take a wife when he is ready."

"I meant no offence, my lord." The sheriff smiled to himself while he scratched away. "Tell me about these knights."

"Hugh of Havering is William's closest man," I said. "He is of an age with William. Fair haired. Men listen when he speaks. Then there is Roger of Tyre. Older but still quick with a blade. Quick of mind and tongue, too. Dark."

"These men have holdings of their own in Outremer," the bishop said, muttering. "Odd that they would follow William de Ferrers back here. Unless they have reason to flee."

"One of the worst is Rollo the Norman" I said, suppressing a shudder. "A vile man who delights in torment. The call him the Beast."

"I have heard much talk of this one," the sheriff said, scratching at his parchment. "The Beast Rollo. He is said to look like a bear."

"A fat bear," the bishop said, smirking. "But hairier."

"And there is Ralph the Reaper who I heard boast of murders he had done in Outremer," I said. "He is supposed to be from some great Saxon family but Hugh of Havering told me he is a tanner's son. And he has Walter who is a little dark Welshman who is quite mad. He rants always that dead men walk the earth. Men who have risen too early for the Last Judgement. Ugly as sin, has wens on his face and your men could not miss him. And of course Hugo the Giant, you must know of him?"

"The giant, yes," the sheriff said. "So he's taller than you?"

I snorted. "Tallest man I have ever seen. Strong, too."

"It is true," the bishop said, shaking his head. "I have seen this man."

"There was never men like them in all Derbyshire until William returned," I said, my voice growing louder. "And they ride away unpunished. If you know of them then you know it was they and not I who did this thing."

The sheriff raised his hands. "We have spoken to the surviving servants. I am sure that it was Earl William and his men."

"His men, yes," the bishop muttered and allowed himself a single tight nod. "Yet I find it hard to believe that Robert's boy could stoop to such a thing. The real question is if there was some purpose anyone might have had in committing these acts."

"We have not been sitting idly." The sheriff leaned forward. "My men ride in all directions as we speak," he said. "If Earl William is hiding in Derbyshire I shall lead my bailiffs there and we shall take him. Justice shall be done, I swear."

"I will go with you," I said and drained my cup, thinking how much I did not want to face William and his knights. But I had sworn an oath.

The sheriff thought for a moment and nodded. "You are welcome to join us."

I felt all the aches in my muscles from digging the graves that morning and lifting and carrying body after body. I had worked beyond the limits of my endurance. I could not recall eating. Peering at the dirt and blood under my fingernails I had to close one eye to focus my vision. My head spun and the most important thing I had to do was to get away from all their questions and judgements and simply close my eyes.

"My lords," I mumbled, heaving myself upright. "I am afraid that I must retire to my wood."

I watched with interest as the floor lurched up to smash me in the face.

∞

Someone slapped me. I was on a low pallet in a small, bare room. It was light outside the high window.

"I'm awake," I mumbled.

The prior slapped me again.

"I said I'm awake, for the love of God," I said, grabbing his wrist.

"You purged yourself upon my floor, young man," Prior Theobald said, yanking his hand back from my grip. He seemed to be considering slapping me a third time.

"Oh, God," I said and covered my face, remembering all that had happened the day before.

The prior's tone softened and he placed his hand upon my shoulder. "The sheriff has returned to see you, Richard." He hesitated. "This is a terrible thing that has happened. All you can do is trust in God. All of us here shall pray for you."

I lay upon my back, hungover and bereft. "Thank you, prior."

When I was young my father had tried to force me to become a monk. My family supported Tutbury Priory so they would take me, unruly as I was. As the second son I may have one day diluted Henry's inheritance. I ran away, then fought and screamed when they brought me back. Earl Robert somehow found out about this and took me into his service instead. Me being a monk would have been like forcing a fox to become a chicken. But our father granted everything to Henry anyway. And Henry gave me nothing.

"It breaks my heart to bring this up so soon," he said. "But your brother had confirmed the Priory's grants when he became the lord of the manor. Sadly, we are yet to receive any of the promised—"

I sat up and pushed past him. "You shall get your grants, Theobald," I said, just to shut him up.

"Thank you, Richard," he said. "My Lord."

I splashed water over myself. One of the brothers led me to the cloister where the sheriff sat reading upon a bench in the centre of the square. Swifts chirped and swooped above and the sun was painfully bright. Two men attended the sheriff. They took the parchments from him and retired to the shadow of the cloister when I approached.

"Where is the bishop this morning, my lord sheriff?" I asked. My mouth tasted like vomit and my head pounded. Nothing I was not used to, of course. At least it was another fine day.

"Call me Roger," the sheriff said, smiling. He looked as

fresh as a daisy, the bastard. "The bishop has more responsibilities than a mortal man can undertake, he tells me. And he rode away last night claiming to be returning to Coventry. Imagine my surprise when I discovered this morning that the bishop instead rode to Duffield Castle. More of his men have ridden up from the south to join him."

"Surely he cannot seize the Earl's castle for himself? Should William be stripped of his lands and title, they are for the king to distribute."

"The king is sailing for the Holy Land. He may even have already left. It seems as though most men of quality are sailing with him." The sheriff sighed. "I have half a mind to take the cross myself. Although I wonder if I would have land and position to return to if men like the bishop are staying to carve up England in the king's absence."

The politics of the realm was of little interest to me. I kept seeing bodies, graves and blood. I had an oath to fulfil. "What of William?"

The sheriff sighed. "I am afraid that William and his men have ridden south for Dartmouth. One of my bailiffs rode back to me through the night. William and his men were seen on the road, dressed for travel. Armed and armoured. That disgusting beast Rollo was heard by my man bragging about getting away with murder and heading for Dartmouth and there to catch a ship."

I had never travelled beyond Derbyshire.

"Surely that is a ruse? Why would he say such things? Perhaps they will take another road?"

The sheriff nodded. "My bailiff said Hugh of Havering battered Rollo about the head for speaking where they could be overheard. My man is trustworthy and I believe him."

"Why did your bailiff not stop them?" I demanded.

The sheriff looked at me but did me the favour of not pointing out the foolishness of my question.

"I must go after them myself," I said.

"I mean no offence when I say this," the sheriff said. "But you will be killed. I doubt you have a chance of besting a single one of any of those men. And together they are seven."

"I was unbeaten in practice," I said. "And I won a melee last summer."

The sheriff held up a hand against my protests. "Of course, of course. But William fought the Saracens in the Holy Land. He was one of the few to survive the massacre of Hattin. And his men sound like the vilest brutes in Christendom. Tell me that I am wrong when I say you will die, Richard."

I did not want to admit it. "Come with me," I asked the

sheriff. "You have men."

"I have no authority beyond this shire," the sheriff said. "What about your friends? The others fostered by Earl Robert before he died. The Levetts have a reputation. Can they ride with you?"

Unsure of how to say it, I hesitated. "I was not well liked," I admitted.

The sheriff frowned. "Ah," he said. "The bishop is convinced that you are a great one for chasing girls. That will make you unpopular."

"I never chased a girl in my life," I said, shrugging. "I don't know why they like me."

"Oh dear. That makes it worse, in my experience," he said, chuckling.

"I always won in practice bouts. Even though I was almost the youngest," I said. "They said it wasn't fair because I was bigger."

"You should have gone easier on them," he said. "That would be the political thing to do. You need allies, Richard. Look at me. I never won a fight in my life and here I am a beloved sheriff."

I laughed. "I should have gone easier, yes. But I enjoyed humiliating them, the bloody bastards. They will never help me with anything."

The sheriff sighed. "In that case, I suggest you do not

throw your life away on a quest that cannot possibly succeed," he said. "That enormous and disgusting man who now goes by the name the Beast Rollo? One of my bailiffs suspects he is from Caen. He escaped a hanging a few years ago by killing the hangman, hacking his way through the crowd and running to Outremer. He truly is a beast. A devil. He should have been killed years ago and many men have tried. I beg you not to go up against men like him. You are a lord now. Stay here and see to your lands."

"I swore an oath to God to avenge them," I said, seeing Isabella's blood welling from her mouth and the pleading in her eyes. "I have no choice but to bring William and those six knights to justice. Rollo included. Hugo the Giant included. If God is just he will lend strength to my arm that I might slay the murderers."

The sheriff shrugged. As well he might. The killers had fled his shire and were unlikely to return. And if I threw my life away chasing after William and his men, well, who was I to the sheriff? He had done his moral duty in attempting to dissuade me but he made another attempt.

We stood. "Go home, Richard," the sheriff said, extending his hand to me in friendship. "Keep swyving Martha in the woods. Take a wife, have some children. Men like William always die by the sword."

"There are no men like William," I said. "But he will die

by my sword."

The truth, of course, was that the sheriff was right. Those men terrified me.

No surviving servant could be induced to stay at Ashbury Manor. It was cursed. I paid some serfs from the village to scrub the blood stains from the floors and walls. I stayed to oversee the work. I was the lord of the manor. The proper incomes from the land would be mine but I could find no steward to manage the work of my own land or gather the rents from my tenants. My standards were low; anyone who said yes would do. But everyone knew that the manor house and my family was cursed by God and to take up with me would curse them as well.

I slept in the wood.

The night before I set out, I rode to Duffield Castle. The bishop was giving a feast with William's meat and bread, in William's hall. The sheriff was there also and I spoke to him at the top table.

"I need a man to look after my land," I said to the sheriff, leaning over to him.

"I will do what I can," the sheriff said.

I knew that when I rode away from Ashbury that I would be riding into penury.

I looked around at the great hall I knew so well. The servants had dutifully served Earl Robert and then served

Earl William. They now served Hugh de Nonant, sitting in the Earl's great dark chair and I suspected they would serve him for a long time. William had left no instructions for the care of Duffield and no man knew when he might return. Indeed, there was no indication that he ever would.

"Richard of Ashbury," the bishop slurred. His mouth dribbled William's good wine and flecks of meat. "Why in God's name are you still in Derbyshire? I thought you were charging off like a bull at a gate."

"I am almost ready to leave, my lord," I said, fighting to keep the anger from my voice.

"I shall pray for your success in hunting down those murderous dogs." He staggered over to me and dumped a heavy purse onto the table.

"My lord?"

"Hire yourself a couple of good fighters," he said, kneading my shoulder and breathing wine into my face. "Or a band of mediocre ones. Give yourself half a chance to be rid of him. If you succeed, I shall give you more."

"Thank you, my lord bishop," I said. He waved a hand over my head and muttered something about God that I suppose was a blessing.

The sheriff laughed at my expression. "Those men deserve the Lord's justice, delivered here on earth by your righteous hand." He held up his wine. "An eye for an eye, a tooth for a tooth and all the rest of it."

I drank heartily to that and then paused. "To apply that principle to William I should have to burst into his home one night and slaughter him, his family and his servants."

"That does sound like rather a lot of work," the sheriff said. "You had better get to it."

I packed everything I needed onto my brother's palfrey – my palfrey now – and went to sleep one last time in the woods.

Almost everyone in the village had ignored me and it was clear they believed my family cursed. But I got one of the lads to ask Martha to meet me in the woods by the stream. That place was ours. It was where we practised the crossbow. And where we practised pleasuring one another.

She came at sunrise. The dawn was clear and hot and the light fell upon her face. Martha had a strong face and clear skin and my heart flew when I saw her picking her way through the trees toward me. I took her hands in mine.

"I have to go away," I said.

"Go then," she said without looking at me.

"I may never return."

That made Martha at least look up. "Who will be lord of Ashbury then?"

"Some other lord, I suppose," I said. Strange to think of some other family taking what had been ours for over a hundred years.

She looked intrigued and then sighed as if she begrudged even speaking to me. "It were right bad what happened to your family, Richard, weren't it."

"I am sorry about running off like this," I said. I assumed she was going to be heartbroken because I was abandoning her. "But you always knew that you and I could never have married. This had to end eventually. You will find a good man from Ashbury to marry. Or from Scropton or even Yeaveley."

Martha laughed, bitterly, twirling her hair. She looked up at me with her huge green eyes. "What you doing with that crossbow?"

I nodded, wondering why I had bothered to say farewell to her. It was not that she was simple and ignorant that put me off her. She lacked even a rudimentary capacity for affection.

"Crossbow? I have no idea what I did with it. If you can find it in the barley near the manor, you are welcome to it, I suppose."

"You suppose? Suppose?" She was angry. "After all I done for you under the oak tree. The least you can do is give me that weapon. And you don't have to be so mean-spirited about giving me what's owed. My dad reckons that a crossbow will fetch a fine price in Chesterfield on market day and I don't doubt he's right."

She was just a girl. Just an ignorant girl and I had been an idiot boy up until William de Ferrers had massacred everyone at Ashbury. But Martha had remained Martha.

"If it's money you are looking for then you should know that the Bishop of Coventry pays his servants well," I said. "You should go see him at Duffield Castle."

I rode south for Dartmouth. If I caught up with William and his knights, I knew not what I would do.

CHAPTER TWO
THE CHASE

IT WAS A FAIR FEW DAYS OF RIDING south and west to get to Dartmouth. I saw more of England in those days that I had in all my previous twenty-one years. The weather turned and once I got drenched, I remained either sodden or damp for a week. At least it was not cold.

The folk at the roadside inns whispered about the group of men who had ridden through before me. A rich man was the leader. Some knew him for an earl.

"Fine-looking man, he was," a stocky old woman said as she slammed a bowl of stew on my table. I was at an inn outside Cirencester and it seemed like she owned the place.

"Just like you, my lord." She winked at me. "Taking the cross, God bless him. But those other men were an evil looking bunch. I have thanked God every night since they passed through that they caused no harm while they were here."

"Didn't you know Edith's little lad's gone missing?" a young serving woman said to her, overhearing.

"That's not got nothing to do with those men, though," the older woman said, scoffing. "What would a band of grown men want with a little boy?"

Others remembered the group passing through at the beginning of spring, heading north. Everyone remembered the giant, Hugo.

"Tallest man in all the world, he was, my lord."

I followed the old road south through hills and across rivers. England was bigger than I had imagined. And everyone was talking about the Crusade. King Richard had spent three years robbing the country to pay for it and he had finally embarked with thousands of knights, mercenaries and most of the great lords of the realm.

That was why asking drunk men in taverns and inns for tales of knights passing by became tiresome.

"Bit late, ain't you, lord?" I was asked about a hundred times. "They left last month."

"The King's in France now, lord. You better hurry or

Saladin's head will be on Jerusalem's wall before you ever get there."

Such is what passes for wit amongst English country folk.

Still, men remembered William passing and when I was closer to the south coast, I knew his destination port for certain.

"And you are sure you heard them say they were heading for Dartmouth."

"They did. But then, he was a liar," an old ditcher with gnarled hands said, sitting behind the great cup of beer that I bought for him outside Shepton Mallet. "They was all liars."

"How so?" I asked.

"There's no Earl in his right mind who would ride in the company of men such as them lot."

"I agree with you," I said. "But he truly is an Earl."

The old man scoffed. "Probably a bloody Scotchman." He knocked back the beer.

I had never ridden so far or for so long and I was saddle sore and weary when I rode along that lovely valley and looked down into that sweet port. My lungs were filled with the salt spray tossed into the wind by the rocky coast.

Dartmouth nestled against a wide river, surrounded by hills green with trees and grazed grass right down to the water's edge. The sea beyond the far mouth of the river was slate-grey to one side and blood red from the setting sun to the other. Between the clusters of ships in the river the water was a glassy silver and black. There was a forest of masts and rigging and furled sails. Wharfs dotted with buildings and men carrying things to and from the docked boats and ships. The men there called out to each other and across the still waters to the ships. It smelled of fish and smoke and life.

I took a room at an inn near the old wooden castle that overlooked the town. After stabling my horse, I descended to the waterside just as the sun fell below the distant horizon. Heart clamouring in my ears I sought out Earl William.

At the inns and taverns, I met indifference, mistrust and downright hostility. I had left my hauberk, helmet and shield at the inn. Perhaps I was making people nervous with the sword at my hip but I saw other men so armed. Perhaps it was because I was an outsider but then I was in a busy port filled with boatloads of strangers.

"We know what you did," one man who was already drunk breathed into my ear in a particularly filthy tavern.

"I have no idea what you mean," I said.

His friends pulled him away from me but their dark looks persuaded me to leave for the next establishment along the dockside, where the welcome was hardly friendlier.

In the last tavern I finally found a merchant with one eye and a hacking cough. After draining the sixth cup of wine that I bought him he told me that William and his men had taken one of his ships just the day before. I sighed, feeling a profound relief flood through me. A relief that I had the decency to feel ashamed of.

"Awful gentlemen, so they were," the merchant said, swaying in his seat. "One of them were a giant. Tall as this room, so help me, God. Threatened me into letting them onto the ship. There weren't the room for them and all their belongings, I told them. Just weren't the room and I begged them but they said they knew where my wife lived. I had to unload twenty four barrels of good salt herring to get them on board, the dirty bastards."

"To where be the ship bound?"

"Going all the way to Marseilles and that's right where your friends wanted to be." He spat on the floor. "The devil take them."

I had heard of the place. "Why would they want to go there?" I asked, almost to myself.

"You can get anything you could ever want there, if you can pay the price," he said, licking his lips and squinting at the jug of wine with his eye. "Pilgrims and the crusaders leave off from Marseilles for the Holy Land. That's where you knights are always heading, ain't it. Any chance of another cup, my lord? I'm right parched, I am. Right parched, by God."

That night I took a room at the inn by the castle. Lying in bed with the stench of the rotten straw mattress filling my nose, I squirmed and itched at the fleabites. As I began finally to drift away, a sobbing came through the walls from somewhere else in the quiet tavern. It betrayed a desperate, inconsolable soul. Instead of sleeping, I listened to that mournful weeping. I resisted shouting for silence.

In the morning, I went to check on the care of my horse. I knew I would have to sell her soon and after a sleepless night, I was in a foul mood.

"Someone in the inn was crying all night," I said to the stable boy, a stocky lad with a dirty face and the stink of horse shit about him.

"If you got something wrong with the rooms you got to tell Old Bert," the lad said, staring at the floor. "My lord."

"I am merely curious," I said. "It sounded like a recent hurt."

He looked confused. "That's just Mags. Joan's mother. Weeping like a spring tide, she is."

"Ah," I said. "And something happened to Joan, I take it?"

"What, you ain't never heard about Joan the Maiden?" the boy said, his face suddenly full of joy.

"I have not."

"She was a girl who works in the inn kitchens. She got found on the banks of the Dart a couple days ago," the stable boy said, full to bursting with importance. "Up at the castle they saying she got her throat savaged by a dog or a bear or something. But that ain't what truly happened."

I saw Isabella, her blood soaking my clothes.

My throat was dry. "What truly happened?"

The boy stopped brushing my horse and lowered his voice. "Folk seen her go off with some rich man that night, lord. But then I heard she went off with a whole group of men. Strangers."

"Why would a maiden go off with a group of strangers?"

"Oh," the boy said, taken aback. "She weren't really a maiden, lord. They just call her that. It's a jest. Because really Joan would lift her skirts for any old—"

"I understand," I said. "So you know who did this terrible thing?"

"No one recognised them," the boy said in a hushed tone. "Which means only one thing, lord."

I assumed he was going to claim they were shape shifters or some form of man-beast because children love such stories. He stared at me so I forced myself to ask. "What does it mean?"

"Jews," the stable boy said and lowered his voice to a whisper. "It was the Jews what done it, lord. They can make themselves look like other men. So me and my brothers are going to set a fire under the Jews" houses tonight. Send them all to hell, right and proper."

"The men responsible have sailed for the Holy Land," I told the stable boy. "A group of men led by a great lord from the north and many here noticed them. One of the knights was a giant. You have no cause to burn the homes of the innocent."

He scoffed at my ignorance, all deference forgotten. "The Jews ain't innocent," he said. "Even if they didn't do Joan, they did our Lord, didn't they?"

I smacked him in the ear hard enough to knock him to the straw.

"I'll get my brothers on you," the sobbing boy said from the ground, his hand over his ear. "You ain't nothing round here, big man."

"Please do direct your brothers to me," I told him. "I will knock them on their arse too, then I will drag them to the town reeve for planning murder and fire setting. Any fires get started in Dartmouth tonight then we shall know whom to hang, won't we. Now, brush down my horse properly or I'll cut your balls off and feed them to the Jews."

That day I watched the ships bobbing in the port and asked for passage from traders and masters. It seemed to me that the town was a mistrustful place full of muttering and unkind looks that turned away whenever I glanced in their direction. But still I spoke to everyone who would hear me.

"Don't take crusaders," one said from his gangplank after looking me up and down. "Sling your hook."

There was one large vessel with high sides, teeming with men. "You cannot afford the cost of a place on my ship," the master said, leering at me as the ship was loaded behind him.

"I am sure that I can," I said, thinking of the silver the Bishop had given me. It seemed a shame to spend it all on a single passage but I was willing to do so. "I will pay whatever it takes."

The master took my elbow and led me to one side, lowering his voice. "The cost is for you to allow me to lay with you, every night, as a man lays with a woman."

I looked at him to see if he was in jest. "I am unwilling to pay that cost."

He scowled, spat at me feet and shoved me aside on his way back to his ship.

Disheartened, I went back to the inn and drank wine until my head span. Across the room from me a group of impoverished young men muttered and stared at me. I grew certain they were intending to run me outside and beat me bloody. I knew not what I had done but I would have welcomed a fight. So I staggered over to them and loomed over their table. One of them leapt to his feet and I shoved him back so hard he fell on his arse and sat there stunned.

"What is it with this place?" I slurred as I spoke. "Are you lads looking for a fight? Because if you are then you have chosen the correct inn for I am rather keen to pummel a man's face into offal." I doubted that the individual words were uttered with any clarity but I trusted that the general thrust would be clear enough.

They were afraid of me even though they were many and I was swimming in wine. "We know it was you what did that to Joan," one of them said.

"Joan?" I spluttered. "What in God's name are you talking about?"

"You was seen," one said, with tears in his eyes. "It was you, clear as day."

"That girl was dead before I even arrived in this goat turd of a port," I said, placing my hand on the hilt of my sword. "Are we fighting or not?"

They declined.

I lay on my mattress that night with the room spinning around me listening to the sobs of the dead girl's mother through the wall. I was certain that William and his men had carried out other murders before Ashbury. They had continued to kill again and again on their way to Dartmouth.

I stuffed my fingers in my ears, prayed to God to give me strength and swore to take any outward bound ship the next day.

∞

I woke late, mouth dry and head pounding and went to the docks and to ask everyone I could about getting passage onward. Dartmouth was heaving with ships. I forced my way through shouting gangs of men and the rising stench of fish as the hot morning got hotter throughout the day. Finally, I heard of a French ship that was ready to leave that night. I was to speak to the sailing master.

That man was Oberto and when I finally tracked him down I discovered that there was no way that he could have been more helpful. For Oberto was an experienced sailor and he knew a young fool with a fat purse when he saw one.

"I hear you are heading for the Mediterranean," I shouted to him after I climbed the gangplank to a deck full of barrels and men. The ship was *La Bon Marie* and it was a slab-sided cog with a huge mast, crisp square sails. She was manned with Frisians, had a French name and owner, was commanded by a Genoese sailing master, but she flew an English flag.

"No more room for merchandise," Oberto the master said, scowling. "Can you not see we are full?" He indicated the barrels and boxes stacked everywhere upon the deck and tied in place. "I cannot stow so much as one more rat."

He was well dressed, dark and reeked of wine. He swayed on his feet though the ship was not moving.

"I am no merchant," I said, full of my own importance. "I must get to Marseilles."

His ruddy face lit up. "A passenger. How wonderful. I am bound for Genoa which is so close to Marseilles they are almost touching." He held up a dirty thumb and forefinger by way of demonstration. "I have a luxurious cabin currently unoccupied and just waiting for you, young man. You are eager to become a warrior of God. You wish to raise your shield in defence of the Holy Land and win back Jerusalem. Well, God has blessed you, my friend, but we must leave this day, on the evening tide."

Because I was looking for one, I saw the destination of the ship as a sign from God. I was eager to make up for my earlier delays and I wished to show the Lord I was eager and willing to pay for my sins. I could not wait to get away from the unkindness of the town and the sobbing of the woman at the inn. So instead of waiting for another ship, striking a hard bargain or inspecting the cabin I ran off. I sold my very fine palfrey for pennies to the innkeeper. He protested that there had been a glut of fine horses sold just a day or two ago and he could pay no more. I then paid half a fortune for what Oberto said was a cabin. I was so ignorant of the world I did not even know to buy my own supplies for the long, appalling journey.

We bobbed out of the harbour that evening as the sun sank on the distant horizon. We headed south into the English Channel, toward Brittany. And once again I was in pursuit of William and his murderers.

"But this is no cabin," I protested.

The cabin in question was no more than a filthy curtain slung across an alcove in the airless belly of the ship. It stank, it was dark as boiling pitch and full of rats. They scratched and scrabbled along the beams. Water dripped everywhere.

"How dare you deceive me, so? I demand a better cabin. A real cabin." The motion of the ship was unnatural and made my head spin and my guts roil.

"It's the best cabin in the whole ship," Oberto lied, grinning. "Even my own cabin is nothing but a hole compared to such luxury as this."

"You swindler," I growled. "You no good Italian cheat."

"I shall be happy to drop you at the next port along the

coast," Oberto said. His smile faltered at my clumsy insults. No doubt he sensed the violent thoughts bubbling up. "Of course, I shall have to retain your payment."

"How dare you, you swindling little swine." I was a whole head and shoulders taller than him and I leaned over him, feeling the anger building within me. "Find me somewhere suitable to bunk or I shall take back my payment and more besides."

He swallowed. "I am afraid there truly is no other place, my lord. The men sleep in hammocks below deck with no more than eighteen inches between them."

"What about your own cabin? Perhaps I shall take that from you?" My threatening tone was immediately undermined by a violent gagging that gripped my guts.

"Please," he said, lowering his voice. "My men would not tolerate such a loss of face for the ship's master. They are a proud crew. They would kill me."

"Then they would be doing me a favour."

"I am the lone man aboard who can navigate. They would put into the nearest port and find a new ship. You, they would have to kill also."

"They can try," I said. I was angry with myself.

"The best I can do, my lord," Oberto said looking down and backing away from me. "Is when we land in Brittany, I will buy a ship's cat to deal with the rats."

I was already ashamed of delaying my pursuit of Earl William. More to the point, I was already suffering from the sea sickness and I clutched the low beam above as my stomach turned over.

I gave in.

There followed many days of vomiting in the dark. I purged myself inside out and after I was as empty as a man could be my limbs and mind were hollow. Despite laying in rotten filth with the stench of ancient bilge filling my nose day and night, I felt cleansed. As if I had left the past behind me when I had departed England.

Of course, I was wrong about that. I had not yet learned that we carry our histories with us wherever we go.

It took weeks of sailing down the coast. We hopped from port to port waiting out storms. Sometimes we were caught in the most astonishingly vast waves. I stayed out of the crew's way and clung to my bunk and every single time I thought that the ship would be sunk. The final storm came as we were closing on Marseilles and we were forced to run before it. Or so Oberto claimed. But we found ourselves in Genoa, many weeks after setting off. By then it was beyond the end of sailing season.

Oberto claimed he was yet willing to sail back to Marseilles but the crew rebelled. The swirling sky above was the same for days on end; a dark smear of roiling cloud, full of storm. To sail out now would be risking their deaths.

"They do whatever you tell them to do," I said.

His eyes twinkled. "Not in this."

"But it is so close," I said. "If we had not met that storm we would have made port there days ago."

"Hmmm," Oberto said, shrugging.

So I bade farewell to the fat little drunkard on the deck of his rotten bucket of a ship. The sailors ignored me and most ran off into the bustling madness of the port of Genoa, no doubt to the brothels and taverns.

"I am so very sorry to see you go," he said, grinning.

"I bet you bloody are, you swindling Italian cheat," I said.

Still, he had been my only company on the ship and I was about to be alone again.

I reached the bottom of the gang plank and dumped my heavy pack and other belongings onto the dockside. Oberto called my name and stood for a moment looking down. Then he yanked the gangplank back halfway where it quivered in the air over the strip of water between the sides and the wharf. He stood at the rail.

"I told you before that Marseilles was this close to Genoa." He held up his hand with finger and thumb pushed together. "But I did not know you, then."

"What are you saying?"

"Marseilles and Genoa? More like this far away." He held both hands out at shoulder width apart.

"You bastard."

I appraised the distance to the rail. The dark water below was full of debris and a film of slime.

"You are a good man, Richard," Oberto said. "You will not hurt me."

In fact it was something like two-hundred and fifty miles to Marseilles, through storm and rain and appalling weather. Few boats risked those conditions and none would take me.

I cursed Oberto's name with every step.

All the while the enormity of my task weighed on me. Finding William somewhere out in the world, which was larger and more terrifying than I had imagined, seemed impossible. Surely, he would not have remained in Marseilles.

But I finally trudged into that grand old city.

And there I found the Beast.

CHAPTER THREE
THE BEAST

I BLUNDERED INTO MARSEILLES before sundown, bone tired and ravenous and looking for a hot meal and a dry bed.

It had taken me ten days to walk from Genoa along the road that ran roughly west with the coast. Sometimes the coast turned north, other times south. But always it felt as though I was going back on myself toward England and away from William.

The landscape of that Mediterranean coast was one of astonishing beauty. I had seen nowhere along the outer edge of Europe to match it. There was coastal plain, mudflats and sand dunes but mostly it was mile after mile of field and forest, dotted with villages and towns. Inland were great hills. The other side, often out of sight, was the storm-wracked Mediterranean. The folk living along that coast were decent enough, though getting them to understand me was sometimes difficult.

Many travellers welcomed me as a companion. Without a horse to carry it, I wore my mail hauberk. I slung my helmet from my pack and wore my shield across my back as I walked so I was sought out as a deterrent to robbers and bandits on the road. Little groups would walk together between the towns. Oftentimes the grateful travellers provided food and wine for me and the other knights and soldiers.

A couple of days out from Marseilles I fell in with an Italian master mason who was heading to the city with his family to build a church. He was in fine mood for, starting in the spring, he would have work for years to come. The eldest daughter was rather lovely and she seemed quite taken with me also. Yet we could not converse and the mason watched us like a hawk when we sat together, smiling at each other and miming.

I reached Marseilles at sundown. It was a dry evening, for once, though everything was soaked and glistening in the sunset. It was a magnificent and ancient place with a vast stone wall and a gateway carved with shapes it. Inside were more stone buildings, some two or even three stories high. Masses of people hurrying about here and there but I was too exhausted to be much aware of it. The air was all smoke, salt, fish and orange sunlight.

Bidding fond farewell to the mason and his family inside the gate – especially his eldest daughter, who winked as she was dragged away – I asked locals politely for directions to somewhere I could sleep and be fed. Some ignored me, hurrying off. Others scowled and cursed me for a foreign devil. I spoke the language of northern France and the city folk spoke the language of the south. I was able to understand them but they treated me as if I was a Saracen.

Oberto had told me that Marseilles was a port city that favoured and welcomed travellers but I supposed that he had lied to me once again. Assuming I would be likely to find a room near the docks I walked toward the water. Some filthy children found me and pestered me for coin until I roared at them waving my arms and they ran away screaming and laughing.

Finally, one man who was fixing nets with his boy directed me down a narrow street.

"Tavern down there," he said, glancing around. "Cheap. Good wine."

I thanked him earnestly.

But it was a trap.

I thought I was imagining that I was followed down that street because when I turned I saw nobody. The street lead to a small square with stone buildings on four sides. It stank of faeces and rotten fish and I could see no obvious way out.

I turned to leave. First six and then a dozen and more men stalked out of the street into the square. They spread out around me. They were ordinary townsfolk but grim and muttering.

I backed away and backed away until I was cornered against the walls of two houses. They stretched up above us and there was nowhere to climb out to.

"Can I help you good fellows with something?" I said, smiling.

They close in on me, still muttering to each other. I saw a wine skin passed around. They stood staring at me. More men walked into the square from the alley which seemed a long way away.

"I can assure you," I said. "That if this is about a woman then I never touched her. I just arrived."

They surrounded me further, swearing and cursing. Some seemed full of wine's bravery and there were many of them. But I wore my hauberk and had a sword at my hip and shield on my back. I was taller than any of them and they would know that a knight is trained from youth in fighting. But I was exhausted and hungry and their numbers and unexplained anger concerned me.

My instinct told me to draw my sword but I knew that there would be no turning back from such an act.

"Where are you from?" a man demanded, pushing his way to the front to stand before me. He was old, about forty and he had the neck and shoulders of a bullock and a red, angry face.

"Genoa," I said, angry at the shaking in my voice. I was a lord, armed and armoured and I would not be afraid of a gang of fisherman.

"He lies. He's not a Genoese."

Others took up the cry. "Liar! Liar!"

"I never said I was born there, I said I just came from there." I looked over the sea of heads. The exit to the square was a long way away.

"He's English," another man said. "He's an Englishman if ever I saw one. His skin's as white as a fish belly."

"Tell the truth or we'll gut you like a fish," the bull-necked leader said. He mimed what I assumed was a gutting motion in front of my face with his meaty fists.

"I am a Norman," I lied. "I arrived in your city mere—"

But my words drowned in the braying of the mob.

"He's a Norman. Another Norman. We found another one."

"Another what?" I shouted, terrified. "Another bloody what?"

The mob leader shuffled near, his face red and shaking with rage. "You killed my wife." He shoved a meaty finger in my face. "You cut out her throat and God forgive me I shall cut out yours in return." And yet he stood and shook rather than attack me.

"I did nothing of the sort," I cried. "I arrived in your city tonight. You can see the dirt of the road upon me. Just now tonight, by God."

No one heard my words. No one wanted to hear them. They were yelling about women killed, about children torn apart.

They prodded and pushed and they had murder in their eyes. But murder is a hard thing for most men and they had not killed me outright, I wondered if there was a way out.

"It was Earl William," I screamed. "William and his men. I am hunting those men myself."

A stout stick hurtled at me and I ducked and it clattered off the wall behind me. And then a jug smashed, splashing dark wine against the wall. They surged forward.

They were going to kill me.

My guts churned. My heart hammered against my ribs pounding in my ears like the sea against black rocks. I struggled to breathe as the hands clawed at me and teeth were bared.

I sent a final prayer to God and drew my sword, intending to slay as many as I could before I was born down.

Different shouts intruded. Barked orders from the rear. The mob before me was drawn back by unseen hands.

Soldiers of Marseilles had arrived.

They yelled and beat at the men attacking me. They forced their way through and stood in front of me making a protective screen and ordered the mob to return to their homes. It took a while and a few of the city folk staggered off with head wounds but they dispersed.

Falling to my knees I thanked God for delivering me from death. I knew then that He was guiding me on my quest.

As I finished my prayers, my saviours gathered me up and beat me into a bloody pulp.

When I woke I was in a gaol. Some frozen black dungeon with no light. At first I was afraid I had been blinded.

Feeling around my body I found that my sword, pack, purse and hauberk were all gone. I lay on a damp stone floor in nothing more than my underclothes. The floor reeked of sweat, mould and the acrid, throat-burning sourness of old piss and human shit. I was already shivering when I woke. My face was stiff with dried blood and my beating by the soldiers came flooding back.

"Awake, are you, boy?" The voice spoke softly but in the close blackness the sound made me jump out of my skin.

"Where am I?" I asked, but it came out as a moan.

"God loves me. Bringing you to me." The voice chuckled. "I saw you. When they opened the door." He spoke English with a strong accent. "I knows you, boy."

The voice was familiar. "Who are you?" I tried to sit up.

Laughter again. Low, deep laughter.

"The Earl was heartbroken that you was not at home. He had plans for you, boy."

Before I got higher than one elbow he scrambled over to me in the dark and pinned me down.

I am a big man and strong. Even then when I was so young but this was a man who had grown into his strength over many years. A man who had filled out with flesh over his muscle and dense bone. I felt his weight pressing down, his giant belly and smelt his stench and I knew who it was.

"Rollo," I said.

One of Earl William's men. That stupid, huge great Norman beast who had murdered his way out of his own hanging.

He laughed again, a low rumbling I felt inside my body.

His breath was rancid as he leaned his face close to mine. "We gutted your brother real nice, didn't we, boy. Oh yes, we gutted him like a trout and he wept when he died. Sobbing like a baby for his poor bit of cunny getting savaged by the Earl right in front of him."

The Beast Rollo thrust his hips and belly down onto my body and I felt a soft-hard rod pushing against my stomach. It could only have been Rollo's enormous, tumescent phallus.

To throw him off I heaved myself up, the muscles in my back and legs straining. But I had no hope. He was twice my weight and he had me pinned on the bare stone floor.

"I cut off your brother's head myself," Rollo said. His lips sounded wet, like he was salivating. "It weren't a quick one, neither. It was a shame but the Earl wanted her ladyship all to his self so he dragged her off to her bed. I would have liked to have seen what he did to her. But I can imagine it pretty well enough, oh yes indeed." There was a wet slithering sound as he licked his lips right over my face.

"Coward," I growled and writhed and twisted. He fell to one side and I got a hand free and punched the darkness where I thought he would be. My fist punched his skull and I nearly broke my hand. I punched his face and neck and shoulder but as I was on my back my blows had no weight behind them. Rollo was a monstrous, fleshy oaf and he felt nothing, grabbed my wrist and pinned me again.

"I been hungry," Rollo said, almost whining. "Please lord, I know he is yours. But I been so hungry. Oh dear me, Christ, I been ever so hungry down here. Ever so hungry. And thirsty." Warm spittle dribbled down onto my chin, neck and lips.

The world turned. And I knew.

I saw Isabella's ripped and torn neck.

The woman in Dartmouth. The wives and children of the mob in Marseilles. The teeth marks on the wet nurse's skin. Their wounds caused not by saws or knives but with teeth.

William and his men were tearing into their victim's living flesh with their teeth. And drinking the blood.

I slammed my head forward, his nose smashing under my forehead.

Rollo grunted. Lifted his head away a fraction.

I butted him again, hard. I felt his grip loosen so I crashed my head forward a third time and Rollo growled, stood and picked me up like a rag doll, dragging me to my feet in the dark.

His fist hit me in the guts so hard I thought I was going to die.

That a blow could hurt so much was astonishing. Unable to draw breath, the panic rose inside me, certain I would suffocate from the paralysis his blow had dealt me. Even as it wore off and I could sense a breath on the horizon, I was certain that my insides had been minced. My guts ruptured. The humours would leak into my body rot me inside out.

I curled upon the floor and as soon as I gasped he kicked me in the face. The darkness burst with silver fire. Some instinct made me roll over and I avoided the next blow. It rushed by my head and I jumped to my feet and limped away as far as I could, trying to control my heaving lungs. I crouched against a damp wall.

Rollo was panting in the dark.

"Where you think you're going to go, boy? He chuckled that deep, low sound. "You're my lovely little feast, you are. You're my lovely little lamb." His feet scraped on the floor as he circled. "Come here, little lamb. Let me taste you."

I slid sideways along the wall, feeling my way with a hand on the crumbly wet stones. If I could just get behind him, I thought, I could knock him senseless. A blow to the back of the knee to bring him crashing down, followed by kicks to the temple until he was dead.

My foot whacked into something solid under foot and a bucket clunked over, spilling a pile of stinking, liquid shit over my feet.

His triumphant growl alerted me to his charge and I

tried to jump to the side.

Instead I slipped in the shit.

He caught me with a glancing blow powerful enough to send me staggering into the wall just as Rollo thudded into it where I had been standing. He snarled in pain and I smashed my elbow toward the sound, connecting with something hard. As he backed away I stalked forward swinging my fists and elbows into his face, his neck, his hands. He grabbed my forearm with a meaty hand and squeezed, bringing me to him.

Instead of pulling away I grabbed his wrist, stepped forward and threw him with my hip. Earl Robert always said the bigger your enemy is the easier he is to overbalance. But Earl Robert, as far as I know, never fought in a black dungeon with his feet covered in slimy shit.

My feet slid midway through the throw and I collapsed with Rollo half on top of me.

We were both stunned. Exhausted by the fight and the fall. His weight had crushed the air from my body. He himself was old and corpulent and he could not catch his stinking breath fast enough. I recovered my breath after a moment but he lay across me, his throat dry and rasping, breathing ragged and hot in my ear. I tried to wriggle out from under him but he pushed my face down and leaned his massive weight on top of me while he got his breath. My head was being crushed, the skin on my face grinding against grit on the slimy stone floor. There was no chance I could lift myself up against his immense force. He may as well have been a mountain atop me for all the use my shaking arms were pushing against it.

So I slid my face along the floor. The skin under my eye scraped into shreds and the flesh of my cheek tore.

"No you don't, boy," Rollo growled above me and heaved down harder. "Where you going?"

It may have been my imagination but I was sure I could hear my skull cracking.

I squirmed my legs up like a frog and shoved myself away further, ripping and gouging my face down to my lips. I got far enough away that his weight was not right above me. It gave me enough space to twist out from under his hand and I lashed out, catching his locked-out elbow with my own. It cracked and Rollo cried out, lifting his body from mine but staying on his knees. I jumped up, ignoring the pain of my bleeding face and grabbed out toward the sound of his panting.

My fingers snaked into his greasy hair and gripped his massive head. He grabbed my wrists but I used my knee to smash him in the face.

It hurt me but it hurt him more. I smashed him again, bringing his face down onto my knee each time. His grip weakened until I was kneeing a wet, crunching mess and his hands dropped.

Still, he stayed upright.

Moving behind him, I got my arm around his throat and another behind his huge neck and squeezed for all I was worth. I ignored the pain in my face and knee.

Rollo reached behind his head and punched me in the face and he slapped and scratched my arms and hands but I held on. He writhed and bucked but I squeezed harder. He coughed out a spray of blood from his smashed face.

He went limp. I squeezed more until I was sure he was not pretending then let him drop. His body hit the stone floor with a thud. I backed away and sat, heaving down air until my heart slowed.

Rollo was not dead. A flicker of life remained inside his vast lump of a body and after a short while he stirred.

"Tough lad," Rollo mumbled, wheezing. "But a week ago I'd have killed you."

I kicked him in the face and stamped on his hands with a shit-covered heel until I felt fingers break and Rollo was hissing in agony. It hurt my foot but it was a satisfying trade.

"Where is William?" I asked Rollo, feeling the tatters of my cheek.

"Gone." Rollo found it difficult to speak with so many teeth broken. His skull must have cracked, too.

"Do not try me," I warned him.

"Gone," Rollo muttered. "To find God."

"Where in the Holy Land has he gone?"

"Back to Acre," Rollo said. "From there to Jerusalem. Where he died and where he was reborn, as the Christ was before him." He chuckled and then coughed blood.

Acre. Earl William was heading for Acre. I let out a great shuddering sigh.

I had a destination.

"He left you here alone?" I asked.

Rollo wailed. "I couldn't stop. He ordered me to flee. She tasted so sweet. The Gift. I wanted it to last. I am so weak." He wailed again. "Forgive me, lord."

"Why, Rollo?" I asked to the darkness, picking pieces of grit from my face. "You are drinking blood? What is this madness that has possessed you all?"

"Madness?" Rollo spat. The sound was wet and thick, like a slap. I thought I heard the hard tinkle of teeth mixed in with the blood. "We are angels, boy. Earl William died and God Himself rose William up. Turned him into the Angel of the Lord. He is the Destroyer. William chose us to share in his gift. We taste of him and we gain his strength. To keep it we must drink. Drink from the Destroyer on God's day. So we each of us drink to stay strong, Sabbath to Sabbath. And we share. We share his sacrament and we become strong. Once we prepare the way he will ascend. Ascend on a pillar of flame to sit in judgement beside the Lord. From now until the end of days."

I kicked him in his huge belly to silence him. He groaned and I kicked him again. I felt him swing at me in the dark so I kicked and stamped down on him once more. Kicking his head with bared feet was like kicking against a rock. But he fell mute again. Other than his laboured and wheezing breath. The foulness of that breath was greater than that of the shit bucket.

If there had been some way to restrain him then I would have done it. I had more questions. But soon he would become dangerous again and I could not share that black cell with him. And I knew that if I allowed myself to sleep even for a moment while Rollo lived then I would never wake.

Instead I prayed that God would see justice in my actions and forgive me if he did not. Anyway, the man was convicted before his hanging. I would be merely carrying out the sentence he had escaped from.

"None but God Himself can sit in judgement, Rollo," I said, standing and stretching my aching limbs. "Which you are about to discover."

"No. Murder. Murder." Rollo cried as I crossed to him once more. "Murder," he roared. My ears rang.

I beat him unconscious and sat across Rollo's back. I got my arm around his neck and pulled upward.

And that was how the guards found me when they threw open the heavy door and blinded me with lamp light.

The guards lifted me from him and took me away. A grizzled old sergeant cleaned my wounds, allowed me to wash, bandaged my face, fed me and gave me a bed. All the while there was a local dignitary and a couple of priests apologising for locking an innocent knight on crusade in with such a monster.

Witnesses including a stone mason had sworn that I had been on the road when the murders had taken place. They said I had entered the city no earlier than the night I was attacked.

"The killings of the women and children lasted for many weeks," they told me. "Soon after the English left."

"The English were here?"

"King Richard the Lionheart and thousands of Englishmen gathered here. They camped to the north. The French, too, led by Philip. The French army was bigger, of course. They left two months ago and then the murders started. A shipwright's wife was taken. Her body found mutilated. More women followed, always taken in the night. Children too. Every man went armed in his own home. Then that one was found asleep in an alley clutching a dead woman and her child to him. They had been cut about the neck. We believed we had our man. But there was another killing the next night while we had this one locked away. No more followed yet everyone thinks another is still out there."

"The other men have fled for the Holy Land," I said. "You can cease fretting."

You are following King Richard the Lionheart, yes?" they said.

"Certainly," I lied.

"When you see him," they said. "Tell him that Marseilles treats Englishmen within the law."

The very idea that I would ever speak to Richard the Lionheart was laughable. "Of course I shall tell him," I said. "It will be the first thing I say."

I gave thanks to God that the good fathers of Marseilles thought enough of justice to let me go, despite what the mob wanted.

The next morning, Rollo hanged.

They let me watch from afar, up on a balcony away from anyone who might attack me. Rollo was still raving about serving the Angel of God while he dangled. With the noose tight about his neck, still he wailed in despair and wept and cried out for William. The hangman had to climb up and clutch onto Rollo's legs and jerk up and down to hasten his end.

The first of my prey brought to justice.
Six more to go.

CHAPTER FOUR
THE LIONHEART

THOSE MEN OF MARSEILLES even returned my sword, helmet, shield and mail hauberk and most of my remaining coin.

"We pray to God that you will forgive us for throwing you in with that devil," they said on the docks. "Take that great cog at the wharf and join your fellow Englishmen, Richard of Ashbury. Never come to Marseilles again."

It was good advice. William headed for Acre. The city of Acre was in Outremer, as us Franks called the Christian parts of the Holy Land, much reduced since the rise of the Saracen king, Saladin. The English were heading for the

Holy Land so I resolved to join them.

I took that Italian ship toward the city of Messina on the island of Sicily. Messina was where King Richard had finally gathered his forces for the crusade. That ship crept down the Italian coast spending days and even weeks in some of the ports while wind and storm kept ships from sailing out again. My face, thank God, healed and there was no scar.

Always I asked after William and his pack of murderers. If I found them I had no way of fighting them all but still I asked. But whichever route they had taken to Acre they had not come my way.

Battling through the last of the bad weather, I arrived in Messina before the Christmas of 1190.

The city of Messina nestled against the isle of Sicily at the far eastern end, opposite the toe of Italy. It was another ancient place, unlike anywhere outside the Mediterranean. A hundred years before I was born the city was conquered by Normans as the first step in the eventual reconquest of the island from the Moors.

Even in winter the sky over that city could be so blue that I would find myself staring up, open mouthed. There were statues everywhere; the marble tarnished and speckled with salt and age but no less impressive for all that. The buildings that surrounded the perfect arc of the bay were of a golden sandstone. The waters were well protected from the elements by a magnificent hook of land that curved out and around so far that it almost closed off the entrance to the harbour.

Philip the King of France was also overwintering in Sicily with his vast army. The two kings had fallen out but they had committed to winning back Jerusalem from the Saracens.

I paid little attention to those high above me. There were two or three thousand English soldiers and knights at Messina. After so long a time in the company of hostile foreigners I was happy at finding so many Englishmen that far from home.

Ragged and filthy and bordering on penniless I was no different from many other knights there. We were second sons and adventurers seeking glory or escape from boredom or from a woman. My father had not been rich nor a very good soldier. Yet a handful of knights remembered Henry of Ashbury as a solid, dependable man and I was acknowledged as the new lord of Ashbury.

Rumour of the nature of the massacre at Ashbury had flown before me and some treated me warily, for a curse is infectious.

No one had seen Earl William. If it had been him alone I was seeking I would have assumed he was disguised, travelling incognito. But his companion was the giant Hugo who could no more hide among men than a castle could hide among houses. So William and his knights had taken another route toward Acre.

Perhaps I should have hurried on ahead before William could get further beyond my grasp. Instead I convinced myself that crossing paths with the English crusader army was a sign from God that I should travel with my countrymen.

And my fight with Rollo had reinforced the impossibility of my sworn task. Against one of his men, a man much weakened by hunger and age, I had barely survived. With the rest, I stood no chance. I would break out in a cold sweat at the thought of facing the terrible power of Hugo the Giant or the lunatic fury of Roger the Reaper.

But the true reason for staying in Sicily was that, within my first week, I saw Alice.

"In the name of God," I said to my new friend Reginald outside our favoured tavern in Messina. "Tell me who is that woman." Many men sat around us, eating and laughing.

The day was once again dry with no more than the slightest chill in the air. We had a good view of the main road through the city. I was content to sit and watch the lords and ladies and servants walking to and fro. We sat between the waterside, the castle, the market and the countryside beyond where some of the richest lords had taken over houses. Children ran everywhere. The English, French and local Normans mixing together as friends and falling out as enemies just as their parents did.

The woman walking down the street with her companions stood out from the world around her like a sunbeam piercing a black cloud. She wore a dark green gown that was demure and respectable and yet it seemed to emphasise every line of her full body beneath. I do believe I gasped when I saw her. I was never before struck in such a way.

"What woman would that be?" Reginald asked, airily.

"You know what one," I said unable to drag my eyes from her.

I watched the way her hips lifted up and down as she walked. She went over to a small group of women in the open courtyard of a large house off the side of the road. Children ran squealing around them. Stray hair fell from all around the front of the woman's cap. Those wisps of hair were as golden and as bright as the dusty Sicilian sunlight. She looked happy. And yet, from the restrained way she smiled at the others who were talking and the way she kept herself apart from the group, I sensed that there was also a sadness about her. A sadness that felt familiar.

In that moment, I wanted more than anything to be able to take her sadness away. Her smile was wide and her lips full. Her face was white but flushed from walking. When she glanced round to light-heartedly curse a child that had bumped into her, I saw her eyes flashing with sudden joy. I wanted to feel the happiness that she felt and I wanted to make her laugh so.

"Do not even think about it," Reginald said wagging a finger at me across the table. "That is Alice de Frenenterre. She comes from Poitou. Her husband was Roger de Sherbourne. He died of a summer fever and he has no surviving relative. She has family in Outremer. Jaffa or somewhere close to Jerusalem, so she's not going back to Poitou."

"Well if her husband is dead, why should I not think about it?"

"The king was swyving her," Reginald said, leering. "Before his betrothed arrived, of course. Wouldn't want the future Queen of England finding out you are a bedswerver. But I tell you King Richard was ploughing her furrow ten times a day."

Reginald was from a wealthy enough family somewhere boggy in Norfolk but he had gone on Crusade as penance for some unspecified disgrace. Over the few days I kept his company I became convinced it had been a crime against a woman. At least one.

"I'd wager that's an exaggeration," I said. I watched her full lips twist together at some joke that had her noble companions suddenly laughing themselves silly. I watched the way she seemed to be the centre of those women's attention and yet a woman with her own mind. Strong enough to not fake a laugh simply because it is expected of you.

Though I had listened to stories of chivalric romance at Duffield. In the few moments I had observed her I awarded to her every virtuous trait in the world.

"She's better than you," Reginald said, intruding into my fantasies. "That is all there is to it. She is several places above you. She's a well-bred lady, from a proper family."

I stared Reginald down. "I am of good stock," I said. The group began to walk through the courtyard toward the door to the house.

"No doubt you top it the lord where you come from," Reginald said, nodding. "But you are piss poor and from some tumbledown shit hole no one outside of Derbyshire ever heard of. But that lady there has royal blood. Or an Austrian cousin married into the Holy Roman Emperor's family. I do not recall." He looked annoyed and drank down his drink, cuffing his mouth.

"It's not her Austrian cousin I want." I could not drag

my eyes from her as she swayed away, her body shifting under her gown, drawing the cloth tight across her hips and arse and chest.

"She's got two children," Reginald pointed out. "A boy called Jocelyn and a girl barely out of swaddling. You wouldn't want to burden yourself like that."

"That's true," I said, staring at her as she finally disappeared from my sight. It was like a light going out. "But it would be worth it."

"But she's ancient," Reginald spluttered. "She must be at least twenty-three years old, Richard. You want to find yourself a nice fresh girl, thirteen or fourteen at the most. Fifteen would do, I suppose, if she's lovely and plump and has good teeth."

"All good advice," I said, turning to him. "You know an awful lot about this lady, Reginald. So tell me, how many times has she turned you down so far?"

"She has never so much as agreed to see me," Reginald wailed. "Whenever I call on her she sends word through some damned servant that she is engaged or out riding in the country. The lying bitch." Reginald turned and spat on the floor. "And if she never saw me then she will never see the likes of you, not never."

Reginald was correct that I had nothing to offer Alice. My land was inconsequential, my inherited manor cursed and my wealth so meagre I could not even afford a proper war horse.

I resolved on the spot to become rich.

"Dear God," I prayed. "I will fight the Saracens in your name. Please grant me glory in battle and riches and let me know that woman's love."

God heard me.

After a few weeks of waiting around, drinking and getting fat, word got about that the storms were lessening. Our winter in Messina would be over just as soon as the weather turned. In preparation for the fighting that was to come I went to get my hauberk properly repaired and the rust scrubbed away with sand and my sword and daggers sharpened. My coin had dwindled in Messina but every penny paid to an armourer was a penny toward the defence of your life. For soon I would be making a name for myself. A name I could use to find William.

I strolled back to my tiny room in the city through the crowded streets dressed as if for war. I had not bothered to purchase a horse I would only have to sell before setting off. There was no way I could have paid for the passage of a horse which could be ten times the cost of carrying me to Outremer. Messina was a lovely city, with wide streets lined here and there with decorative olive and lemon trees. Even under Norman rule and packed with stinking knights from the north, it retained an air of exotic luxury.

A young boy ran hard into my leg and fell down on his backside.

The boy looked to be about five or six years old and he looked up in fear until I winked at him. The boy grinned.

He had been playing Knights and Saracens with a much bigger boy. A boy who proceeded to stomp over and yank the little one up by his ear and clout him about the head.

"You stupid oaf," the big boy said. He had the idiot fat face of a noble. He was carrying a real sword, forged small enough to fit his hand. I hated the child on sight. "If you go running into a man during a real fight and you will die upon the battlefield. You die puking your innards out into the dust. You will be crying for your whore mother while you bleed all the blood out of your body and shit yourself to death."

The little one looked furious and close to tears in equal measure, gripping his little wooden sword to his chest as if it were a doll.

"Don't listen to him," I said to the younger lad. "He's never been on a battlefield in his life. He's talking out of his arse. Why don't you try fighting me, then, you horrible little twerp?"

The younger boy grinned up at me again.

"How dare you," the fat one shrieked, his face turning a

sickly scarlet. "How dare you speak thus, you ignorant peasant. Do you know who I am? Do you? I shall have you executed for this."

"And do you know who I am?" I asked him.

The boy stuck out one of his chins. The top one. "Tell me your name," he commanded.

"Get out of here before I rip your guts out," I said and knocked his sword down, spun him around and kicked his arse hard enough to pitch him onto his belly. Men walking around us laughed and he ran away in tears to the sound of jeering.

"Bohemund will be angry," the little boy said as we stood watching him go.

"Well, I had better teach you how to fight properly then, hadn't I," I said.

He nodded solemnly, his eyes huge and round.

I ripped a spindly dry stick from an olive tree and we fought a few mock battles until he had killed me two or three times and was smiling from ear to ear. "Right, be off with you, lad," I said. "And stay away from fat Bohemund. I know his type. Get some better friends."

"He's not my friend," the little lad said, with a viciousness quite startling in one so young. "I hate him. Mother says I have to play with him so that I have proper acquaintance when he inherits."

"What's that fat shit going to inherit?"

"Sicily."

"I see." My guts churned over. "And what's your name, lad?" I asked.

"I am Jocelyn de Sherbourne," he said.

"So," I said, the name catching me off guard. "Your mother is... Alice?"

"That's her up there," Jocelyn said and pointed to a figure in a high window above the street looking down at us. She was bareheaded and those golden hairs blown by the wind caught the sunlight like sparks from a flame. I locked eyes with her and I saw the corner of her mouth twitch upward.

She invited me inside for refreshments. There were other ladies in the room, of course, and we conversed of topics that held no interest for me. Just being near to her made my heart race and I could not meet her eye for more than a moment at a time. I mumbled and stumbled my way through and I was certain that she thought me an utter fool.

"It would please me if you were to return tomorrow evening," she said as I left. "But perhaps wearing something more suitable." She laughed at me. I felt a true horror when I looked down and realised that my hauberk was not appropriate dress.

"My lady," I said, ready to offer a thousand apologies.

She laughed again and pushed me out. "See you tomorrow, Richard."

We met a few times and each time I grew more comfortable in her presence until I could hold her gaze. My heart still raced to be near her.

Soon enough, one day as I left she placed her fingers gently upon my arm to delay me at the door. She whispered up at my ear as I bent down, her breath upon my face.

"Return after dark."

The sweetest words that ever were spoke.

There was a strange feeling among the army and the followers while on Crusade. It reminded me of the high excitement of the shire fair or a celebratory holy day, when all of the normal rules are suspended for the duration. It was as though we existed outside of the true world. Love affairs bloomed and died many times over between men and women who would never have conversed in England. But we slept in strange houses in strange cities in strange countries. It mattered nothing if the servants or local people saw goings on. We would be gone from those places before the whispers could do damage. Coitus outside of marriage was against the law, against God and against common decency and it was so ingrained that most couples ensured they were discrete.

"People will talk," I whispered to Alice in the night.

"Not if we are careful," Alice replied. Even when she whispered, her voice sounded as though it came from deep inside of her.

"The men look on me with loathing," I said proud beyond words that they suspected where I had been spending my nights.

I heard the smile in her voice. "Think what the women say of me. Taking a lover in my widowhood. They say I am mad with lust." She pinched my chest. "And they speak truth."

Neither of us were breaking any vows spoken in the sacrament of marriage but it might blacken her good name.

"Should we not marry?" I asked.

Alice sighed. "And what happens to me when you are killed by the Saracens? Twice widowed in my youth. No man shall want me for fear of death."

It was a strange answer. "I know that I am very much beneath you," I started to say.

"You are beneath me," she whispered in my ear and slid her leg over me and sat up across my loins. "Right where I want you."

It was April 1191. We had spent the coldest nights of winter in each other's arms and every day of spring we knew our time together was coming to an end.

When the fleet set off from Sicily I saw her no more.

I swore to her on our last night together that I would think of her every day and every night.

"I know you will, Richard," she said.

The fleet spread out over hundreds of sea miles, calling at the ports of Italy and Greece on different days. Being apart from her felt like a blade through the guts. I could not wait until we reached Acre. I was going to win back the Holy Land single handed and become a lord and marry Alice and we would raise some fine boys. Boys who would become knights and make us proud with fine deeds. And I would ride down William and his men from the back of my horse. I pictured a huge grassland and two dozen knights in service to me riding with me. We would dispatch William and Hugh of Havering and Ralph the Reaper and Hugo the Giant and the all rest to Hell with a lance to the spine. Such are the fantasies of a lonely young man.

Alice was in the fine, seaworthy ship that carried the future queen whereas I was slung inside a rotting sponge that had once been a galley. The only reason it floated at all was because woodworm are buoyant.

And yet when the great storm hit, the royal ship that Alice and her children were in ran aground upon Cyprus whereas ours survived to limp on to Rhodes. I thought the ship from Dartmouth had been through bad weather but it was nothing like that storm. The wind seemed to come from every direction, one direction after the other and the waves were a chaos of choppy great peaks. When it passed our galley was so low in the water that should a single man on board have sneezed we would have immediately rolled over and sunk.

The Byzantine ruler of Cyprus had treated King Richard's shipwrecked family discourteously. There was a rumour that Richard's sister and his betrothed were kidnapped, or threatened or imprisoned then released. Whatever had happened, it was a serious affront to his authority. Richard the Lionheart dealt with challenges by charging at them headlong and battering them into submission.

He decided to conquer Cyprus.

I feared that Alice was hurt also and I threw myself into the conquest.

"Don't get all worked up about this stuff, son." A knight said to me while we crouched behind a field boundary wall. We were awaiting the horns sounding the attack. We were going to capture the city of Limassol on the south coast of the island. The walls of the city bristled with defenders and we were close enough to smell them.

Cyprus was hot; hotter even than Sicily had been and it grew hotter every day. When the sky was not full of storm it was blowing up dry dust and scorching heat. I shared the last of my water with the knight beside me so he felt as though he offered me something in return. Sadly, all he had was advice.

"The king's wife was never in any danger. That was an excuse. Richard has planned to take Cyprus for years. Ever since he took the cross back, three years ago. Or is it four now?"

"How do you know what the king planned?" I asked him.

"Everyone knows," he said.

"I did not know," I replied.

"And who are you, son?" the knight asked, scoffing. He was old, forty or so, but he looked tough. And he had a good point.

We picked up the long ladder along with half a dozen other men and ran forward under a hail of crossbow bolts. Limassol's ancient walls stood defended by thousands of men and we were hundreds. But our leader was Richard the Lionheart.

I was fighting for a chance of a life with Alice. I was fighting for riches enough to fulfil my oath.

So I was one of the first to scale the wall. Stones and arrows pelted my shield. It is difficult to scale a long, unsound ladder under such conditions. But I reached the top, threw myself over the crumbling wall and drew my sword.

The first man I ever killed died by the thrusting point of my sword entering his throat. His blood gushed out onto the dusty wall and mixed with the blood of the men dying around him as my fellows reached the tops of the ladders all along the wall. He was very slim, with a short and trimmed beard and I watched as the man died, his eyes wide and confused, as if he was shocked that this could happen.

I did not know those men. If I had never arrived on their island they would have never done me harm. If I had held back in the rear ranks as many knights do then I would not have had to kill them. And yet I was screaming with a mindless hate as I hacked down the defenders on the walls.

They fell back. Into the edges of the city, between the walls of houses, we found walls of men arrayed against us.

I had been training for war since I was seven years old. Day after day of grappling, riding, sword, shield, footwork. Thirteen years of practice and it finally became useful. My sword was like lightning flashing in a cloudless sky. I hacked up and down on shields and hammered at men and clashed against their raised weapons. I watched myself ducking and swerving around blows, as if every other man was blind and I alone could see.

But all the rage I had saved up over that time came pouring out. All my grief and fear and I lost myself in the fighting.

It is a strange to experience the part of you that is your reason, your goodness and your soul sit to one side. You watch the animal rage take control of your body.

Somehow, I cut my way through a line of Byzantine soldiers. I found myself far from my companions, cut off and surrounded by the enemy. I had no choice but to keep moving through the city. If I stopped moving I would die. I kept laying about me, cutting and snarling at anyone who came close. At some point, I lost my shield.

I was finally trapped down a narrow street. The faces around me twisted in anger and fear but they hesitated. My sword dripped with blood onto the dusty street. Blood and chunks of flesh drenched my hauberk and surcoat.

I had time to wonder whether my own men had abandoned me intentionally. I had been lost in my rage and could not remember what had happened. I waited, sweating and attracting flies. They were afraid to attack me. And no wonder. Soaked in the blood of their friends, I must have looked like Satan himself.

Shouting filled the street behind them and the Byzantines ran. There were Englishmen everywhere, slapping me on the back and laughing. Soon, cheering started.

The old knight from before the battle found me

afterwards. He threw his arm about my neck as we walked through the streets of Limassol.

"What was your name again, lad?" he asked.

Later that day the king himself approached me.

I sat on a low wall with my head in my hands before the administrative building near the highest point in the city. The man sitting beside me jabbed my ribs with his elbow and dropped down to his knees. When I looked round I saw that everyone else nearby was kneeling.

King Richard stood over me, smiling down with regal condescension. Dust and red sunlight filled his fair hair. His face was sunburned red but otherwise it was fine and full of heartiness. I remembered that he was said to have lain with my Alice and I felt a moment's desire to run him through.

Instead, I knelt.

"Get up, lads," the king said. His voice was loud, friendly and clear as a summer sky. "Richard of Ashbury? Stand up, son."

He called me son, even though I was over twenty years old and he was barely into his thirties. I stood. Few men were of a height with me back in those centuries but Richard was able to look me straight in the eye.

"I heard you charged right through their lines," he said, chuckling. "And you kept going and they chased after you, leaving the way open for the rest of us." He laughed a full-throated laugh. "And you went running all the way to the palace and the bloody idiots chased you all the way."

"I didn't know what else to do," I said.

The king threw back his head and roared with laughter. His men, some of the greatest men in Christendom, laughed with him.

The king raised up my hand my hand before our tired army and called out to everyone around.

"Listen up, boys. This is Richard of Ashbury," the king yelled. "The knight who won us Cyprus."

Everyone laughed and cheered. The truth was I had gone charging off like the arrogant, idiot boy I was. If the enemy had been of quality I would have been hacked to pieces in moments.

But at least my blundering had caught the attention of the king. That was the start I needed to speed me on my way to a fortune.

For soon we would make the short voyage from Cyprus to the city of Acre on the coast of Outremer, long besieged by the Saracens.

And it was beneath the walls of Acre that I would find William.

Alice sent for me. Later, we lay in her bed in her new apartments in Limassol.

She stroked the tips of her fingers down my face and whispered into my ear. "If you continue to win such favour from the king then you won't be beneath me much longer."

"Then you would marry me?" I asked, as subtle as a kick to the face.

She sighed and stretched out like a cat. "The Holy Land presents great opportunity for a man who can fight."

"I shall fight well," I promised. "I shall win renown. When I have enough men I shall find William and bring him to justice."

Alice scoffed at my quest for vengeance. "William de Ferrers is a great lord," she said. "He could have dozens of men, perhaps a hundred."

She was quite right, of course but I had no wish to hear reason. "I have no quarrel with any men other than those who massacred my brother's family."

Alice sighed. "You think those other men will stand idly by while you kill their lord? Or that the other great lords who are his friends will allow you to get away with murder?"

"It would not be murder," I started to protest.

"Yes, yes," she said, running her finger over my bottom lip. "But justice to you will seem a crime all its own to those bound to de Ferrers."

"I care not," I mumbled, petulant and irritated by her good sense.

"If you were my husband," she said, making my heart race. "Would you not care that your crime would destroy my reputation also? And darken that of my son?"

In truth, I cared little for Jocelyn then, who was nothing but a reminder that Alice had loved and lived with a man well before I had slunk into her bed.

"Well, what am I to do, then?" I snarled, sitting up away from her.

"Precisely as you are doing," she said and drew me back down.

We landed at Acre in June 1191; almost two years after the struggle for the city had begun. King Guy of Jerusalem had surrounded the city entirely. Saladin and his vast armies were in turn besieging the Franks for all of those two years, cutting the Christians off from the rest of Outremer. The sea there was the bluest thing I had ever seen and sun was hotter and whiter even than in Cyprus. But it stank. It stank of the sewage from thousands of men who had encamped and been trapped for such a long time.

King Philip had arrived weeks before us but his thousands of Frenchmen had no impact on the struggle. It was a mighty tough city; well protected. Acre sat on the coast at the end of a short peninsular. The landward side blocked by two great defensive walls dotted with towers.

Only when King Richard and the English landed did the Franks mount any serious assault on the city.

I did not find William.

There was little chance to move about amongst the besieging armies. The English were on one side of the peninsular, the French on the other. Between were the forces of Jerusalem and the barons of Outremer. I asked after William and his knights but I could find no word of them. It was a huge disappointment as well as a relief.

The Holy Land presents great opportunity for a man who can fight.

So I put myself in the thickest of the fighting. For a month I fought for the walls. I climbed ladders and manned siege towers while under desperate attack from the garrison. There were thousands of Saracen knights inside the city but they were still merely a tenth our number. Still, they fought with the knowledge that losing the city might mean their slaughter. Many of the Saracens had their wives and children with them. I have no doubt that without those families to protect the garrison would have surrendered years before.

We also came under attack from outside where Saladin redoubled efforts to crush us before we could retake the city. I fought there, too, manning the palisades with my shield held high to block the endless shower of arrows.

Outremer was nothing like Messina or Cyprus. The feeling of a country fair was long gone. The social rules were not suspended. If anything, they became amplified in the cramped, hungry camps and ships. Jealousies raged and petty scores settled between men and women who were sick of the sight of one another. I could not see Alice. I knew that nobles and wealthy knights were wooing her with promises of security and a bright future for her son.

Often, I thought of my brother Henry. He never spoke of his time in the Holy Land, not in the whole time between his returning home and his death at William's hand. But I imagined him here, fighting and wondered if he had fought well, or even fought at all.

I killed many Saracens at Acre. But there were thousands of other mad, prideful and ambitious Englishmen and I did not stand out from the crowd.

A month after the English landed, terms were agreed and Acre was handed over to the Franks. We took the brave Saracen garrison and their families as prisoners. Saladin was to pay a vast sum of gold in exchange for their freedom. But Saladin delayed his end of the bargain. Payment was promised by a certain date and then he would beg for more time when that day arrived. Saladin was gaining time to build up his forces while the Franks ground to a halt at

Acre, unable to take advantage of our victory.

All Saladin's previous Frankish opponents had been weak. But Richard was not like those other men. Common decency, fairness and charity were as nothing when compared to King Richard's lust for greatness. Since his youth he was known as the Lionheart and he had a lion's instinct for violence.

Richard ordered that the three thousand Saracen prisoners - all of the men, many of their women and even some children - be taken to a hill in full sight of Saladin's camp.

And there be executed.

We knights imagined that it was a gesture to force Saladin to pay up so I made sure I volunteered to carry out the act. It was a confusing jumble of shouting and angry Christians and Saracens who gathered outside the walls of the city. Everyone poured out to watch, unable to believe that Richard was truly going to do it. It was a scorching day and the sun burned my skin.

We marched the three thousand prisoners to a low hill just a little way from Acre across the stony plain.

And there, in full view of the Saracen armies and with Saladin's distant banner fluttering above them all, we cut off three thousand heads.

The prisoners lined up in columns, stepping forward to

the row where they had to kneel and have their heads struck from their bodies. The screams came down the line as hundreds of us began hacking into the kneeling prisoners. The first few hundred bodies were dragged away but then those men gave up because there were so many. And the bodies piled up. The dusty ground became saturated with blood.

The Saracens accepted their fate. Some stood silent, many prayed under their breath as they shuffled forward. Just a few wept and sobbed. I saw none at all trying to fight or escape and although to do so would have been useless, it struck me as strange that thousands could be so utterly resigned to their terrible fate.

Sergeants walked up and down behind us, shouting. "The king wants every head cut right off. So do it properly. When did you last sharpen that blade? Go get an axe, son."

A young man, emaciated from captivity, knelt before me. He was mumbling a prayer and his brothers were cut down either side of him but he did not shake. I sent my own silent prayer to God and hacked down. My blow broke his spine and he died immediately. But King Richard had ordered three thousand heads be cut from three thousand bodies so I hacked it clean off.

By my third I could no longer see through the tears and my hands shook too much to continue. Men willing and able to take my place jostled me aside, sloshing through the blood and laughing at the madness of it all. To work up the will to do such things many men had drunk themselves halfway senseless. It felt like something between the joyous anarchy of a village fair, a battlefield and the fervour of a special mass. It was as though we had allowed ourselves to lose our minds

The horror of that day was like nothing I had ever seen and have rarely seen since. Three thousand necks pumped blood out from their bodies in arcing spurts. If each Saracen lost as little as three or four pints of blood then we had shed well over a thousand gallons of the stuff. I watched it pouring over that hillside, running in rivers down the sides into gullies, pooling in hollows and soaking into the dry earth.

I staggered away shaking and covered in blood, stepping over the dead and dying, the screams ringing in my ears.

And there was William.

Earl William, as bloody as I and standing there clear as day.

Through the press of soldiers and prisoners he was staring at me as if he had been waiting for me to notice him. He was grinning. His teeth red with blood.

William wiped chunks of flesh from his face. And then he sucked them all up into his mouth, chewing and swallowing them down.

Roger of Tyre, one of his most loyal men, brought William a cup and he threw it back. Blood poured down his cheeks and neck. He cuffed his mouth and smacked his lips, tossing the cup back to Roger who laughed and went to get more.

I looked around but no one else seemed to notice the knight gulping down the blood of the enemy like it was wine. But then, who could possibly have noticed such a thing? The only Franks upon that hill were drunk madmen intent on hacking even women and children in two.

Around the hill were groups of mounted knights and ranks of crossbowmen who stood ready to defend us should the Saracens decide to break the truce and attack. The distant armies of Saladin seemed to be working themselves into a fury of vengeance and it seemed as though they would soon attack. No doubt our knights would share my disgust that an English Earl was drinking human blood and even eating raw human flesh. But none of them would have helped me take him.

William saw me looking all around and he laughed.

"We do God's work, my dear Richard," William shouted, his voice powerful and clear through the screams of those dying and the prayers of those waiting to die. William sucked more blood from his fingers and licked his hands.

His knights were with him. They were nudging each other and jeering me. Hugo the Giant towered over them all, his face as blank as it ever was.

"I killed the Beast Rollo," I shouted.

They were surprised. William, I thought, was impressed. The others were angry.

I readied myself, loosening my sword arm. Surely they would not attack a fellow knight where all could see?

Men fell all around us and the blood flowed underfoot.

William smiled and spoke to his men, who laughed.

"Who's looking after your whore, Richard?" Hugh of Havering shouted.

"Should not leave a lady undefended, my lord," Roger of Tyre cried. "I hear there are bad men about."

I turned and ran through the blood back to Acre, their laughter ringing in my ears.

∞

Their threats were nothing more than mockery. Alice was alive and well inside the walls of Acre.

But they knew about her. She could pay no knights to stand guard over her and so I raged at her to flee to somewhere that she could be safe.

"I will not run," Alice said, scorning my fears. "What could he possibly do to me here? I am under the protection of King Richard."

We were in her living quarters. She had ordered the servants from the room when I burst in straight from the massacre. It was a fine, compact home that she had found. The city and a smear of sea was out the window over her shoulder.

She was under the protection of King Richard. "And everyone knows exactly what you had to do to gain his protection."

She pierced my heart with a look of contempt. "I shall not defend my actions to you."

Running to her chambers to find her alive and her children playing had given me such relief that it took me a while to understand why she was angry. As far as the nobility was concerned, she and I could have no reason for being together whatsoever. Charging into her home crying her name was idiotic. It was dangerous to her position and her continued good name. If that name was ruined, if she was known to be having intimate relations with a penniless knight, a powerful lord could never marry her without himself becoming tainted. Rumours could denied but common knowledge would be a disaster.

We had not lain together since Limassol and I knew that she may never lay with me again. But I was willing to risk my own happiness and her future position if it meant she would understand that William was dangerous.

"I am so sorry that I said that," I said, although I wasn't. "But even the King may not be able to protect you."

"And you can?" She looked at me with such pity that my soul withered. "I never realised what a child you were until this moment."

"You do not understand." I strode across the room and loomed over her. "William is evil."

"Evil? I know what is happening outside the city. Is that not evil?" she said, backing away from me. "I know that you demanded a place for yourself. Tell me, how many women did you kill before you came running to me? How many children?"

"I killed merely a few soldiers," I said, wincing. "Saracen soldiers. Killing them is no sin, the Pope has said so. And anyway, I did it for you." I told her proudly, like a cat who brings home a dying rat for its owner.

"For me?" She recoiled further toward her window. "How dare you associate such an act with me? Do not sully me so. What you did, you did for yourself. You love killing, I have seen your eyes shining when you speak of battle."

I was shocked. "We decided that our one chance of

being together was to win favour with the king. It is my only hope of bringing William to justice. But my victories in battle come to nothing," I said, pleading. "I needed to prove to King Richard that I was willing to do anything for his crusade. That way he will remember me when it is time to hand out estates when the Kingdom of Jerusalem is restored."

She shook her head. "No, Richard. No, he will put this massacre out of his mind and it will be as if it had never happened. And any man who reminds him of this will never be close to him again. Did you see any great lords out there upon that hill? No, of course not. They are all with the king, feasting and pretending this is not happening. No, I am afraid that you have quite ruined your prospects."

I was about to demand how she could know the inner workings of a king's mind but then I imagined her and him in Messina before the king's betrothed arrived. Alice and Richard, entwined in a vast bed, him whispering whatever it was that kings whisper. It was like a knife to the chest.

I thought of all the nights Alice and I had spent laying in her bed whispering to each other. I'd had my share of frenzied humping in the woods or castle storerooms but those moments with Alice were my first experience of intimacy. Yet she had shared countless quiet, special moments with both her husband and the King of England before me. Perhaps with others.

A young man's heart and his sense of worth are the most fragile, pathetic and useless things on earth and mine shrivelled up like a worm on a drystone wall.

"Please, Alice, promise me you shall protect yourself from William," I said, lowering my face to hers. "No matter how you feel about me. Promise me you shall never be alone with him or allow his men to approach you. Never be alone anywhere. And keep your children close."

"Richard, get away from me," she said, her nose wrinkling.

I saw myself in her wide, shining eyes. I had washed the worst of the blood from me and had put on fresh clothes. But my hair stuck out wildly from the blood that I had not washed away. I could see my own drawn and wild face staring back at me.

"I am sorry." I held up my hands and backed away from her. "I am sorry for everything. Alice, I beg you, do not go near that monster nor any of his men. If you do nothing else—"

"Leave," she said, pointing at her door.

On my way out, Jocelyn stared up at me with a hurt and fearful expression. I should have ruffled his hair or bid him a good day. But I stormed right by him without a second look.

William had been with the French forces at Acre all along, keeping his men quiet and well out of the fighting. But they could not resist that massacre.

I did not know what to do about William. And there was no time to think about it. Immediately after the massacre the entire Frankish army along with our women and children were marched south along the coast.

We were marching for the port of Jaffa. Once that fell we would retake the Holy City of Jerusalem.

William and his knights marched with us.

CHAPTER FIVE
RENOWN

JAFFA WAS SEVENTY MILES AWAY south along the coast. The huge Saracen army that had surrounded us while we won back Acre matched our course further inland. They mirrored our advance and harassed us with attacks by their light cavalry.

Our infantry marched on the inland side of the road in tight formation. Outside of them were our crossbowmen who warded off the Saracen cavalry. Safe inside near the coast was the baggage train.

I rode with the mounted knights between the baggage and the infantry. I spent the last of my silver on a steady black mare before leaving Acre. Good horses were hard to find in Outremer and the prices were enormous. Most knights rode a destrier, a war horse trained in the forward charge and the richer knights had two or three held in reserve. I had no chance of buying a destrier so my mare was merely a rouncey that had once belonged to a squire. She was too old for war but she was all I had. Because she was black I called her Morel and I took care of her and prayed she would survive the march.

Off the coast, our fleet matched us and shipped food and supplies and took off the wounded and sick.

The Knights Templar lead the way as our vanguard and the Knights Hospitaller guarded the rear; the two most vulnerable positions.

King Richard was lord of vast and diverse lands and it was the Poitevins, the Bretons and the Angevins who marched behind the Templars. The English and the Normans and the forces of the Kingdom of Jerusalem marched behind them. The king rode his golden horse up and down the lines often with his huge retinue of lords and bodyguards. He was keeping an eye on us all, ensuring that we stayed together. But also he shouted encouragement, told us what was happening and reminded us that we were led by a man who knew how to lead.

Behind the English were King Philip's French and the

local barons of Outremer, as well as all the Germans and Austrians and all the other Christians who were with us.

William, as a lord of Outremer holding land in the County of Tripoli, rode among them with his men.

I did not know what to do about William. No king or great lord or bishop would have paid me any heed had I made accusations about William and his crimes in England and elsewhere.

For many nights I imagined creeping through the darkness to where he camped and slitting his throat. I would have to move silently and to do that would require ridding myself of hauberk and helmet. Even leather creaked so I would need to go unarmoured. I would take no more than a short sword or even a dagger. I would blacken my face and my blade with ground charcoal mixed with oil and slip through sleeping forms until I found him. I pictured sawing my blade back and forth across his throat, the blood bubbling out with his screams.

His men would wake, of course. They would cut me down in moments. But at least my duty would be done.

I was too much of a coward to do it. It was easy to convince myself that I would likely fail before ever reaching William. I would be discovered before reaching William. Even if I could find him in the dark amongst so many thousands of others. And if I failed there would be no one to stop William from killing Alice out of spite or whatever madness it was that possessed him. I told myself that I was willing to die for my oath, for justice and vengeance but I did not want my death to be certain.

We marched and rode for many days through the intense heat and Saladin's cavalry harassed us without fail on every one of them. We marched in full armour and the roaring heat claimed many of us, fainting away into shaking madness and death.

But still we did not hurry.

At the Battle of Hattin five years before, the Frankish knights had marched right into a land with no water. Their true battle had been fought against the heat of the desert. Saladin had lured them that way and the fools had fallen for it. And that was why the combined Christian forces were slaughtered almost to a man. Without thousands of knights to protect the Holy City, Jerusalem was ultimately lost and thousands of good Christian people sold into slavery by Saladin. And so King Richard had us march only in the cooler mornings, rising before dawn to march from water source to water source. I thanked God every day that we were led by a king with common sense rather than by the fools who had blundered out to Hattin.

The women rode in carriages and covered wagons by the coast in the safest part of our army. Alice was one of them, along with her children. I could not see Alice but my thoughts were with her. I had soured her feelings toward me and any distant hope I had of marriage was dashed. And yet again and again I heard William's man shouting to me across that hill of blood.

How's your whore?

The thought of Alice being rent asunder as Isabella had been drove me mad on that march, more even than the baking sun did. William could attack during the march and I would be too far away to do anything. We had to stay in our formations. If men were allowed to move up and down the column then our entire strategy could fall to pieces. I was bound to stay where I was but would William would not consider himself bound by such orders.

At least the baggage train and precious supplies - including the women - were guarded by sober and vigilant men. And William must know that to commit such a crime, even if he escaped, would ruin his name throughout Outremer. But then he had thrown away an entire Earldom in England so he was utterly mad and perhaps cared little for self-preservation.

And so we marched. In ten days we came to a vast woodland; a precious rarity in the low coastal regions Holy Land.

The Wood of Arsuf was not the familiar lush, bright

green woods of England. It was an astonishing mix of dark green pines and cedars with black bark. There were wild, gnarled olives, whole groves of scented bay and strange local oaks, like the English kind but different. Unknown and familiar birds chirped and flitted about above. After so long exposed to the scorching sun that wood was sweet relief.

But feelings of peace never last.

Whispers of the coming ambush sped up and down the lines. Always on the march the Saracens had ridden along our landward flank. But once we reached the woodland they now lurked in front and behind, tightening the noose about us. We were cut off in front and cut off behind. The single thing protecting us from slaughter was that we kept tight together.

"They are forming to attack. No matter what they attack with," Richard told us as we approached the southern end of the woodland. "We must all hold until they have exhausted themselves. And keep moving, always together."

At Hattin, the Saracens had weakened the Franks with endless storms of arrows and javelins, goading them into the knight's charge. But once the Franks had expended their devastating charge they were cut down and destroyed. Earl William had been at that battle and had been one of the few to survive and escape. I prayed for William's death in the coming battle.

"We hold until they exhaust themselves," Richard shouted as he trotted past us. "Wait until six blasts of the trumpets. We hold and hold until with God's will we will destroy them in one glorious charge. We hold and then charge on six blasts. Remember Hattin."

The Saracens burst from the trees with a cacophony so daunting it was as if the doors of hell were opening before us. They pounded vast drums and clashed mighty cymbals and gongs. They blasted hundreds of trumpets and the wide swathe of horsemen and infantry screamed and bellowed their war cries.

I had never been in a true battle. I had fought in sieges, stormed walls and taken towns and I had killed so many men that I had lost count. So I thought I knew all there was to know about war. But I was mounted, behind ranks of heavily armoured infantry and still I shook. Already sweating freely I was hit with a sudden chill and the need to evacuate my bowels.

The Saracens charged forward on foot and on horseback and the first of them launched thousands of javelins and darts into our men.

The javelin men on foot threw their missiles and pulled back. The mounted forces launched theirs and they too retreated back into the edge of the wood where more horsemen streamed forward.

Our infantry held up their shields and those missiles thudded into the heavy wood like thunder. Some found their way through the shields and the hauberks and helmets and the first cries of the wounded and dying began.

We moved forward a few dozen paces and formed up again as the dreaded horse archers thrummed a thousand arrows into us every few seconds. Our crossbows clicked and thronged, their bolts felling the man or horse whenever they found a target.

The Saracens had more men and they had more arrows. But their arrows were smaller, lighter and lacked the power needed to penetrate our men's mail hauberks and thick doublets beneath. Soon I saw many of our men marching with one or even half a dozen arrows sticking out from their backs or shoulders. There was no time to stop and remove them from the armour. But any arrow can find the gaps in armour. If a shield is not raised in time an arrow will smash through a man's face like a knife through a boiled turnip. Many of our men had rents in their hauberks from previous battles and arrows found their way through. Our wounded were helped inward away from the fighting.

Swords are as light as air but holding up a shield is tiring. Even for men trained to it and as the day wore on we lost more and more men to the relentless arrow storm.

We knights were itching to charge out and take the fight

to the Saracens. We were close behind our infantry. Should Saladin send his heavy cavalry then we had to be ready to counter it. Instead we walked our horses or held them steady as the arrows rained down upon us, too. The mounted knights were as well protected as the infantry and usually more so. But we lost many horses. Some got hit in the rumps and led away toward the coast and baggage train with hopes for recovery. If a knight did not have a spare mount he went forward to join the ranks of the infantry.

King Richard was everywhere, riding up and down with his loyal knights surrounding him. "Hold, men, hold. Stay together. They shall not break us. God is with us, God is with us." His throat rasped and no wonder for he had been bellowing encouragement for hours and thousands of feet and hoofs had kicked up clouds of fine dust.

My horse, my precious, sweet black Morel, took an arrow in the neck. It went through one of the big veins. The poor beast reared only a little and stood bravely while I dismounted. Then she bent her legs and went down slowly, blood pouring from her muscled neck. I thought of Isabella.

I held her head and looked into her huge dark eye. "I am sorry, girl," I whispered in her ear as I drove my sword up into her skull.

I grabbed my shield and pushed forward through the crossbowmen towards the infantry. I had no wish to fight on foot but I was too poor to have a spare mount or a squire to look after it.

"For the love of God, Richard," I heard Henry of Champagne cry out. "Let us run them down."

"You will hold," King Richard roared, yanking his reins close behind me. "Remember Hattin." The king was attended by dozens of knights and lords and I scurried out of their way.

I wondered if I should run back to the baggage train to guard Alice. The madness of a battle was just the kind of situation that Earl William could use to get to her and her children. Holding my shield up high over my head against arrows raining down, I peered back through the thronging mounted knights behind me. I wondered how I could get away from the front line without being accused of cowardice.

The man next to me was laughing with his friend when an arrow struck him through the cheek, slamming down through his mouth into the back of his head. He was down and thrashing like a fish on a hook and hot blood gushed out to drench the man. Mouth wounds bleed profusely and the ground beneath him was soaked. But he did not die right away. His friends dragged him to his feet and walked him back through the massed horsemen. They went toward the coast where the wounded were thrown onto wagons to die or, if they were wealthy, be cared for.

I looked down at myself. Horse blood soaked me. If discovered, I would be ridiculed and perhaps condemned and ostracised but still I decided I would feign injury for long enough to get to the baggage train and then check on Alice. Once I knew she was well I would return to fight. It was worth the risk to my reputation.

"Richard of Ashbury." The king bellowed my name and I jumped from my thoughts, terrified he had known my intent. "Where is your mount?" He was pointing his sword right at me and shouting over the heads of crossbowmen and through milling horsemen.

"Dead," I called back. "Arrow."

The king knew I was nothing but a poor knight. But he knew I could fight like the devil and he needed warriors that day.

"Give this man a horse," King Richard shouted at one of his men and turned back to me. "You ride with me."

Men around me looked on me with admiration, jealousy and hatred. I crawled upon my new horse's back. He was a very fine destrier, one of Henry of Champagne's spare mounts, no less. I rode after the King and his retinue back down the line to where fighting was even fiercer. I rode among kings and princes and famous knights and was out of place with my cheap armour and faded, battered shield.

But I would never have a better chance of making a future for myself.

The rear of our forces was suffering an all-out attack. Saladin was throwing his entire right wing at the Knights Hospitaller. And as fine soldiers as they were they were being slowly crushed. It was madness. Arrows darkened the sky and men shoved and pushed and screams filled the air. Banners of all colours and designs danced back and forth above it all. The Saracen army was endless and stretched over a mile or more from our lines to the trees and more came to join the press of men and horse. The Hospitallers were being surrounded and pressed back.

And then there he was.

William rode toward me through the madness. He was wore black-painted mail under a black surcoat with a white cross and a black helmet with a black shield and white cross. I shook my head to clear my vision, as surely William would not be riding to speak to the king of England.

But he was riding alongside a black-helmeted lord who I knew was the Master of the Order of the Hospitallers. It was the Master who rode back to address Richard. And William rode with him.

As they reined in, I was surprised to see King Richard glance between me and William. I had not known that Richard was aware of William's crime but of course rumour had reached him. The other nobles looked to me, too.

"We are being destroyed," the Master shouted as his horse slewed to a stop. "My knights, my men are being cut to pieces and you do nothing."

William yanked his horse's reins, jerking the poor beast's head so hard I thought its neck would break. My enemy caught my eye and his lips spread outward into a reptilian grin.

"You will hold," Richard shouted back at the Master. "Or I will pray that God damn you, my lord. Stay together and hold until all their forces are close and committed. We have but one chance to catch them all."

"They are not committed now," the Master said, waving at the scene. "If we do not charge immediately we shall be lost."

William laughed. "Perhaps that your desire?" He spoke to King Richard. "Perhaps you wish to be rid of the good Hospitallers? You want no challenge to your own control of Outremer, is that not true?" William laughed again and glanced at the Master of the Hospitallers who simply scowled at him in return.

Richard's men cried protests but the king silenced them with a look.

"William de Ferrers," the King of England said, his face twisted as I had never seen before. The king was angry. "You are a murderer."

"Aren't we all?" William said grinning and indicating the battle around us. The nobles around me cursed him again.

"He is my man," the Master interjected. "He is convicted of no crime."

"I am his liege lord," King Richard said. "But no longer."

I could not believe what I was hearing, it was as though God had begun answering my prayers.

William spat. "I shall never return to England." He had found a new protector and new brothers in arms by joining the Order of the Hospitallers.

"This is irrelevant," the Master said, in something approaching a wail. "My men are dying. The best knights in Christendom are dying and it is your fault." He thrust an accusing finger at my king.

"Saladin's horses are lighter and faster than ours," Richard explained, with astonishing patience considering the Master's disrespect.

While he spoke, William and I stared at each other. His eyes were burning with intensity. Arrows and screams fell all about us.

Richard continued explaining to the Master as if we were on a training ground not a battlefield. "If we charge too soon they shall pull back from us until our horses tire. They shall turn and slaughter us while we are separated from our soldiers. We must suffer and die until they have exhausted themselves. Then we shall catch them." Richard rode close to the Master who put his hand warily to his sword. "My lord, if we catch them when they are close we will crush them all. We can recover Jerusalem for Christendom if only we hold. Until the signal. Six blasts of the trumpets, then you may charge and win back the city of Christ in a single stroke."

The Master looked almost convinced but still desperate. William, his eyes flickering between me and the king, walked his horse sideways a step and leaned in toward the Master, speaking quietly. The Master nodded once, he wheeled his horse about and charged back to his dying men.

William gave me a final grin before scything his reigns hard and rode off after the Master of the Hospitallers.

"Saladin's banner," a knight shouted. "Saladin himself is there."

"Is he correct?" King Richard shouted to his men.

"It may be his, sire," one of the barons said. "Or his brother's."

"If it is Saladin," the king said to one of his barons. "Then he means to break us here."

"Perhaps we should charge after all," Henry of Champagne said from next to the king.

"Not yet," the king said, irritated. "We are in no true danger."

"Yet we have lost so many horses I wonder if we will have enough to make a deadly charge," the mercenary lord Mercadier said. "We have to flatten the bastards."

A huge cry went up on our left.

The Hospitallers were surging forward and bellowing a battle cry. "Saint George!"

They roared it over and over and hundreds of horsemen were galloping from the ranks of infantry into the Saracen forces.

"Damn him," King Richard shouted. "Damn that man."

The Master of the Hospitallers was leading the charge into the Saracen horses, who were indeed pulling back away from the charge.

It was William who made that charge happen. But even I admit that the Hospitaller charge was glorious to behold. They formed ragged lines as they rode, drawing close to charge knee to knee forming a wall of man and horse and armour, lances couched and deadly. When they reached forces who could not ride away the crash of arms on armour and flesh was loud enough to wake the dead. Unmounted Saracen archers and javelin men, lightly armoured and packed tightly together. Pinned by the thousands behind them were crushed. When their lances stuck fast into men or shields they were dropped and swords and maces seized. The Knights Hospitaller, released finally from hours of suffering, began to pay back what they had received.

"Shall we call them to retreat, sire?" Richard's men asked.

The king stared at the horsemen. They would soon be surrounded and cut off and I thought the king was going to sacrifice them. If they could not obey orders then let them die, I thought. It's what I would have done.

"Sound the attack," Richard cried. "Our whole line, every man, all-out attack. Destroy them!"

The trumpets sounded six times, the signal repeated again and again all along our line.

The Hospitaller foot soldiers had begun their charge even before the king had ordered the trumpets to sound. They were the first to reach their mounted knights and they ran right into the Saracen counter attack.

The French knights and the barons of Outremer charged by us through their infantry into the Saracen centre and the men ran after them to support. The ground shook and drummed louder than a thunderstorm. The trumpets sounded and cymbals crashed and men bellowed the names of their lords and favoured saints.

Saladin's banner fluttered at the rear. King Richard stared at it across the thousands of men and horse. Saladin had committed heavily but not yet completely. The Saracens were restricted by the weight of their own men at the back who did not know to flee but here and there gaps began to open in their lines and their mounted archers began to slip away.

King Richard had no need to fight. Our counter attack had stunned the Saracens and we were carving our way into them. But he loved to fight and he believed a king should fight and lead by example. He was raised in a chivalric court and so he grinned at us over his shoulder, raked his heels back and charged into the battle for the centre.

We rode hard with him. I was in grand company.

"For the Lionheart!" Henry of Champagne cried on my left, his lance tight under his arm.

"God wills it!" the Duke of Burgundy shouted.

I had no lance but I extended my sword and charged into the massed ranks of Saracens. The press of men was terrifying and arrows cracked into helmet and mail. Dust kicked up everywhere and the sweat ran into my eyes, half blinding me. I hacked down again and again. I found myself with enemy on all sides. Swords stabbed up toward me and hands grabbed at my legs and feet, trying to heave me from my saddle. I stabbed and hacked. My horse was trained well in the ways of war and he snapped his teeth at the men about him and kicked his feet back and raked the air in front as I tried to clear a path and keep moving.

A gap opened on my left and I was fighting toward that gap when King Richard charged into it, away from his men and thrusting deep into the Saracen lines.

His barons, his bodyguard, his household troops were cut off from him and shouting and pleading for him to come back. Those men laid about them trying to reach him. They were the finest warriors in Christendom and they loved their king dearly but the mass of men and horse was so dense that even when horses were killed there was no room for them to fall over.

Mercadier, Richard's beloved chief mercenary roared and battered friend and foe alike to force his way through.

"Save him," Henry of Champagne shouted at me with tears in his eyes.

For I was the man closest to the king.

Other lords and knights took up the cry and shouted at me to bring him back. They begged and in their voices were the tears they were shedding at the thought of his death.

I fought harder and urged my horse on toward the king. My sword arm was numb from use and there was little strength left in my blows. Earlier I had been crashing my blade into helmets so hard that the men beneath fell from a single blow but it was all I could do to keep my arm rising and falling.

The king was so close I could hear the juddering of his breath. The sound of a man close to collapse from exhaustion. A huge, armoured Saracen knight on a heavy war horse forced his way between me and the king. He had a magnificent great beard and a face like an eagle that showed no fear. Whether he recognised the king's lion shield and coat or just knew he was a lord worthy of a fine prize, it was clear he wanted to take the king. Yet he knew he had to deal with me first so he swung his curved blade into what remained of my shield. The man's blows were powerful and swift and he hacked it into splinters in moments while I held off attacks from behind me. I gripped hard with my knees while my horse kicked and bucked.

The last of my shield was smashed away and I stabbed my sword through into the armoured Saracen, catching him by surprise and piercing his head under the ear. I sawed my blade back out and blood gushed everywhere and he slumped over still trying to fight.

I looked up in time to see king pulled slowly from his saddle down onto the ground.

Pulling my feet from the stirrups I got my feet underneath me on the saddle. As I crouched, my horse had his guts torn out. A spear was stabbed up into his belly and dragged back and forth and the destrier screamed and tried to rear up in the cramped space.

I leapt from the saddle across the dying Saracen knight and fell down where the king had fallen.

The fall stunned me.

Beneath the press of men and horse it was dark and airless. The ground drenched with blood. Richard was dazed and two Saracen bowmen pulled him away by the feet. Another furiously yanked at the king's helmet.

They wanted to capture and not kill the king. Some men shoved each other trying to get at him. Others stared up, no doubt at the king's bodyguard cutting their way toward him. Those Saracens hesitated, edged back into the throng while those behind could not push through to reach him.

Stabbing up with my sword, I cut into the man trying to steal Richard's crowned helmet. It was easy to push the blade into his kidney as he wore no armour. Crawling over the king I pushed him down into the drenched ground and bullied the other two away from him. On my knees, slashing wildly above I flung the king onto his back to check how badly he was wounded.

The blood made it impossible to tell at a glance but his eyes were open, though unfocused. He may have been stunned or dying.

Above me, the Saracens were closing in again, blades and bows being used as clubs smashed into my back. I felt ribs break and catching a single breath was hard. A powerful blow rang my head and I staggered upright, swinging my sword all around and driving away the crowd to make a space about us.

I never saw the spear. The Saracen who thrust it into me must have been strong. It pierced the mail outside my left forearm, tore through the muscle and then the mail on the other side of my arm, rent the hauberk again and lodged deep into the bone at my hip.

What a shock that blow was. Incredible, pinning me against the king's horse who snapped his teeth at me. The Saracens roared victory and charged forward for the king who was gaining his feet. Blinded by the agony I staggered forward, scything my sword back and forth. I clove a man's hand in half down the middle. I bashed an archer's jaw from his face. I narrowly missed striking the king's head from his body. They attacked me, someone grabbed the spear in my side and twisted. The agony brought me to my knees. My lips snarled back into a grimace so tight I felt them split.

Hooves drummed on the earth and I knew we were dead. The Saracen knights had reached us. I threw myself across the king and blindly batted away the hands that reached down.

A voice and hot breath in my ear. "They are friends, Richard. They are friends. You have done your duty."

I was flat on my back. Shapes moved above.

"Have him healed," the voice said. "Mercadier, bring me your surgeon. I want this brave man treated as if it were me under the saw."

"Do not take my arm," I begged but the noise I made was a moan and no one answered.

CHAPTER SIX

LOSS

TIME PASSED. THERE WERE MOMENTS when I thought I must be in Heaven but then I would feel agony lancing through me and I knew I was not dead. There were flashes of faces and sensations. I was burning hot and another time I was washed with cool water. A woman sang to me. A great lord stood over me asking questions of someone I could not see.

Please do not take my arm.

"Is he awake again?" A woman's voice said. It sounded familiar. "He's mumbling."

"His wound has not festered," the physician as I came

to. He was prodding my hip through stiff bandages that reeked of vinegar. "The fever has passed." He did not seem happy about my recovery. I could tell he was a proper physician because he was old and arrogant and he seemed offended by the very existence of my body.

I reached up with two arms and looked at both my hands. One was bandaged all around the forearm. They had not removed my arm. A great sigh poured out of me.

"Where am I?" It was daylight but I lay in shadow. A hot breeze fluttered the yellow walls of tent. There was blue sky beyond the flapping canvas.

"Do not attempt to speak," the physician said, peering down at me. There were other men behind and about him. On a long table I saw glass jars, bowls of piss and blood and leeches.

It was Alice who then spoke. "Surely his swift recovery is a miracle?"

The physician scoffed. "Ha." Which I believe was intended to convey what he thought of God's intervention on earth compared to his own medical abilities.

"Alice?" I looked for her.

"I am here, Richard." Her face appeared over me, smiling. Behind her were two of her ladies that I recognised from Messina.

I knew that time had passed since the battle but the last

clear thing I remembered was being skewered with a spear. "What happened, Alice, with the battle? Does the king live?"

She laughed softly and patted my arm. "You ask that every time. You were gravely wounded, many times over, saving the life of the king. He is extremely grateful. But your wounds healed, miraculously."

"It was no miracle," the physician said, intruding. "In all likelihood it was simply a matter of receiving a superior standard of medical attention. In all likelihood."

"What happened?" I asked. "How did I get here?"

"Leave us," she commanded the physician and he bowed to her and backed away, waving his hovering attendants with him. They huddled in the corner of the tent throwing irritated glances back at me.

"How are you?" I asked her. "Your children?"

Her face lit up brighter than the sun outside. "We are all well," she said. "You are sweet to ask."

"Did we destroy the Saracens?" I said. "What has happened?"

She laughed. "The battle was won, my darling. We could have destroyed the Saracens army if only those stupid Hospitallers had not charged too early. But it was a great victory. They were beaten badly and have pulled back to Damascus or wherever to lick their wounds. And so we took back Jaffa really quite easily. So everyone says, I did not see anything of it, thanks be to God."

"It was William," I mumbled. "Earl William started that Hospitaller charge. Where is he? Why in God's name was he riding with the Order? Did he survive the battle? Has he been seen?"

Her face clouded over at the mention of his name and I thought I had erred in bringing him up. "Since the battle everyone has been talking about him. He was with the Hospitallers because he lost his lands in the County of Tripoli for some dark crime. He swore his service and the service of his men to the Order. I suppose they did not realise what they were accepting. After the battle he did another great murder. He slaughtered a group of Saracen nobles. They were valuable prisoners and he did it in some bloody fashion that grows with the retelling. People are saying that he drained their blood into barrels so that he could drink it like wine. Isn't that absurd? Anyway, Earl William has taken flight once more. The king declared his lands in England forfeit. The Hospitallers have disowned him also and even sent men to hunt him down but he eludes capture. It seems you were right about him. And everyone of note agrees." She smiled again, a sudden brightness. "But he is gone, do not concern yourself."

"He is gone," I repeated. "Praise God."

"They told me you would die," Alice said, her mouth drawing tight. "Then they said they would have to take your arm before infection set in but I commanded them to wait. Then that it would take you months to heal. They know nothing."

"How long have I been here?"

"A week? Yes, seven days, or eight. So much has happened."

"Where is here?"

"We are in Jaffa, in the grounds of my house. The servants are clearing all the Saracen nonsense from inside. And the doctors said you required air that is fresh."

"Your house?" I did not understand how we could have moved from such disagreement and bad feeling to me being welcomed, I assumed openly, into her household. She was chaperoned by her ladies but still it was strange. I lowered my voice. "I had assumed we would not see each other any longer. Not like this, at least."

"Like this?"

"Me laying under you so."

She smiled but I saw pain in her eyes. "I thought I had lost you," she whispered. "When I heard that you had fallen I thought that I would never see you again." She looked away for a long moment and sighed before continuing. "You are a fool, Richard. An uncouth, ignorant blustering great fool with no clue how to speak to a lady."

"I am."

"But I cannot imagine spending my life with anyone else." She smiled again and took my hand. Her fair skin had been darkened by the sun since I last saw her and her hair was even fairer. She was so beautiful that it took my breath away.

"What do you mean?" I said.

"You sweet fool, Richard. The king has granted you an estate here in Palestine, not far from Jaffa," Alice said, her huge eyes shining over me, her face ringed with golden locks lit from behind by the glare of the sun. "Now we can be married."

∞

The king did not attend our wedding. In truth, it was a rather modest ceremony. But a few nobles from across Christendom were there in the small, beautiful church of Saint Michael near Jaffa's harbour.

They wanted to have my acquaintance. For I had saved the life of the King of England by defending him from uncounted enemies and an otherwise-certain death. And I had done so alone and done it so successfully that the king was hardly wounded.

Over wine and at table the king had sung my praises ever since, for it was a good story and he told it well. He had me granted land. A home that had belonged to a lord who had gone mad with homesickness and returned to Burgundy. My liege lord in Outremer was the King of Jerusalem. King of a city held by the Saracens but the kingdom included Jaffa and Acre and so I was a man of standing. And my dear, brilliant wife Alice was content. Her children had protection and stability and she had me.

The war was not over. Saladin was beaten but far from broken. The lords and kings pressured the sole remaining leader of the crusade, King Richard, to push on from Jaffa toward Jerusalem. The Knights Templar and the Knights Hospitaller told the rest of the Franks that we would never hold Jerusalem. We would be unable to protect the supply line from Jaffa if we took it. But the Hospitallers remained out of favour for their brash charge, even though they had denounced and run out the instigator. And the great lords and the archbishops needled Richard into attacking anyway, convinced that God would give them victory.

Twice we got so close that we could smell the Holy City. It stank to high Heaven. But we were driven back. First by appalling weather that winter of 1191 and then, when the deluge had ceased, by the squabbles between the lords of Outremer. They despised each other far more than any of them despised the Saracens.

By the second attempt on the Holy City both sides in the war were exhausted. After so many years of constant warfare, even the most battle-hardened and war-mad knight had begun to lose his will to fight.

Saladin and Richard loved war at least as much as they feared God. But by 1192 both men seemed to lose their famed energies. Both seemed willing to accept that though neither had won, neither had lost, either. Both men were also pulled away from the war by internal political problems back in their homelands. Richard was hearing whispers that his brother John was plotting to steal his throne back in England.

The King and Saladin negotiated over the winter and well into the spring but still the war dragged on without resolution.

My wife and her children moved with me to my new estate. In truth it was a somewhat sad little place, much abused by the war but Alice set the servants to work in that way of hers and in a few weeks it was repaired and cleaned and comfortable enough. With my new estate I had income enough to keep four men of my own to fight for me. They would ride with me in battle and guard us while we slept. Franks who had fought in battle and were said to be trustworthy, sober men. Four tough men were enough to protect against petty thieves and perhaps even a middling level of banditry. More importantly, I finally had men to scrub my mail, oil my leather and carry my shield.

It was strange to find myself with a complete family. But I enjoyed it immensely. Emma was a joy because she was full of life and devoid of fear. She was always bringing us every horrific, giant thing that crept or slithered or crawled that she could find for half a mile of our house. I was terrified that she would be killed by some venomous foreign evil thing that she presented to me as though she had discovered the greatest jewel in Christendom.

"Stop worrying," Alice would say and laugh at me. "She knows which are the dangerous ones."

I was astonished that a three-year-old child could have such knowledge. "Which are the dangerous ones?"

"Whichever do not run away, of course."

When I looked at Jocelyn charging about with his wooden sword, his stocky body and fair hair were a vision of my brother Henry from when I was young. Thoughts of Henry lead immediately to the memory of holding his severed head. And fearless little Emma was a vision of Isabella's little girl Joanna who last I saw as tattered skin and bloody bone. My thoughts ran always to William, intruding upon my happiness. I hated him for that more than anything

So I could not rest. I could not be happy, not ever, until I fulfilled my oath.

I looked for him. I went to Jaffa and asked after him. Many knew of his treachery and everyone told the same story; that he and his men had slaughtered a dozen Saracen nobles held in the chapel of Saint George. The prisoners had belonged to Henry of Champagne and he was furious. And then William and his knights had slipped away after the incident.

William was lord of an estate up in the County of Tripoli, granted to him after some service long forgotten before Hattin. I looked for him there.

The steward was bitter and ancient. "He ain't here," he said, his voice creaking like dried leather. "My lord ain't been here for years and years."

I got the impression that the steward was not unhappy about his masterless existence.

"Where else might your lord be?"

The steward shrugged. "In Hell, I hope."

"My liege lord is Earl William's uncle, back in England," I lied. "I have been sent to bring the Earl home for he has inherited a magnificent castle. There will be coin for the man who united me with William and your lord will be thankful to you for telling me."

The steward never told me anymore, pleading

ignorance. I was unsure whether to believe him but knew not what more I could do to get the truth out of the old man.

Still, I used the same lie or variations of it all over Outremer in the hope that someone, somewhere would reveal the truth of William's location. That whiff of reward meant I heard many stories from men who would say anything for a dream of silver. The truth was I had exhausted my ideas and pitiful gambits and I had no idea where to look next.

"You are wasting your life and your strength on an old promise made to a dead Aragon whore half the world away," Alice accused me after I returned from a long foray to the north with Otto, the oldest and steadiest of my men.

"And you are jealous of a dead woman," I said, angry at her because what she said was true. "My brother's wife, who I never so much as touched."

"You love her more than you love me or else why are you out there all the time instead of at home with your wife?" Alice said, her eyes filled with her fire.

"You know why," I said. "I owe it to my brother."

"Oh, your oath. Your famous oath," she said. "You do not even have affection for your brother. What about your oath to me, sworn before God? What about what you owe to us?"

What could I say?

"And," she said, knowing that she had me on the run. "What if you are called upon to fight while you are away in the north? And also you do not leave enough guards to protect us when you are gone."

I could no more resist Alice than the sea could resist the moon. She did not have to compel me for I wanted to give up. I never forgot my oath; I simply ceased to act upon it.

And so we had a year of something approaching bliss. We delighted in each other. I belonged to a place and together we were a family. A home of my own and one that had no connection to my father. A home I had won through my own efforts.

A beautiful woman who shaped me with her love and wisdom and discourse. I recognised that my infatuation with Isabella had been a childish fantasy based on nothing more than her exotic mystery. Isabella had been an idea for me, a metaphor for the promise of the great and strange world out there beyond the close horizons of Derbyshire. The lady had shown me kindness and courtesy that was so unlike the simple coarseness of the other girls I had known. Isabella had been a bright bird flying into my drab hall and I was a puppy staring at it, wanting it but not knowing what I would do if I ever caught it.

Marriage to Alice was real. As real as the earth beneath

my feet and the sun upon my face. My wife opened my eyes to what sharing your life with another person could be like. She saw me feeling happy and sad and she saw me raging and reflective and still she looked at me with tenderness in her eyes and a smile upon her lips.

"Do not stare at me so," she said as she dressed one morning, smiling and covering her heavy breasts. "I have the body of an old woman. Your lust is unseemly."

I grabbed her, then, and pull her back into bed. Her body was full and round and strong and it made me lightheaded just to stroke her pale skin or to grab a handful of her warm flesh and breathe her in.

"Be gentle," she said and then hesitated. "I may be with child."

I whooped and leapt up and span her round and round.

"Be gentle," she shrieked, laughing.

All I had ever been good for was fighting. I had no idea how to assess my income or dispense justice. Alice tried to teach me but I am afraid I was never a good student and she took care of most of the estate management day by day while I did my best to keep up with her and learn by watching the adeptness with which she handled our tenants" disputes and our neighbours" scheming over dinner.

Her children would never truly be mine but I felt I was becoming an adequate father. Whenever he wanted, I instructed Jocelyn in the rudiments of armed and unarmed combat and taught him English words that for some reason he found hilarious. Some of those occasions where our serious training dissolved into laughter are among the happiest and most blissful moments of my long life.

The girl, Emma, was as full of joy as it is possible to be. She delighted in stories and would happily listen to anyone willing to tell her tales. Although she remained somewhat afraid of me, she began climbing into my lap in the evenings and sleeping there because she knew I would never allow her to be sent to bed once she did so.

It was its own reward but was also good practice. For soon, I would be a father to a baby who would be truly mine.

Of all the hundreds of years I have lived, 1192 was one of the best.

Often since then I have asked myself how I could have continued to underestimate William. I had seen the depths of the evil that he was capable of. I suppose it was just so much easier to pretend otherwise.

They came in the night.

They always do.

Something woke me. I sat up in bed listening but there was

nothing but the wind against the half-open shutters and Alice's soft, steady breathing. Disturbed by my movement, she mumbled and rolled over next to me, her body under the sheets a series of waves edged in moonlight.

One of my dogs barked once and then fell silent. Sometimes they would bark themselves into a frenzy at the hyenas in the night. My huntsman swore it was because lions roamed about us in the dark, though I had never seen one. But a single bark was unheard of and the fact that neither my huntsman nor his son was shouting at the dog to be silent sent shivers down my spine.

I slipped from the bed and went to the window. The moon was bright and the sky clear and I could see out across my land. I had no significant defences, merely thorn hedges and stone walls to keep wild animals out and my own animals in. The wall of the stables was picked out clearly but I could hear nothing. A horse snorted and whinnied and then I knew that thieves had come. I took down my sword from the wall, silently cursing my useless bloody men for failing to post a proper guard.

The hills of Palestine could be cold at night but I was naked and looking for something to pull on when the screaming started.

It was a throat-shattering scream of agony. Whether of man or woman was hard to tell.

The scream, undoubtedly, had come from within our house.

"Stay here," I said to Alice. But she leapt from the bed and ran naked by me toward the children's rooms down the corridor, her feet slapping on the tiles.

Planting my feet in the corridor I stood guard while she gathered the confused children into her arms.

"Take them back to our chamber," I commanded her and she trotted back with Jocelyn on her hip and little Emma held to her shoulder.

"Where are your clothes, mother?" Jocelyn asked as she dumped him on the bed. Emma was rubbing her eyes.

"What is happening?" Alice asked me.

"Thieves," I said. "Perhaps raiders."

"Let us flee through the window," Alice said to me. "Take the horses and ride for Jaffa."

"They are already in the stables," I said, looking out. "I shall discover what is happening. Get dressed and wait here for me to return."

Fateful words but I believed them to be for the best.

Another scream pierced the night.

"They are in the hall," I said, guessing but sure I was right.

The children looked terrified, clinging to their mother.

"Let the men earn their keep," Alice said. "Stay with us."

"What kind of lord would I be if I allow thieves and robbers to attack us at will?" I said.

She hugged her children to her and nodded.

I ran back down the corridor. In my haste I had still not dressed.

A man in a black surcoat rounded the corridor. He carried a torch in one hand and a mace in the other.

It was Walter the Welshman. I knew him as a nasty piece of shit who terrorised the women and girls of Ashbury after William had brought him back from the Holy Land. As ugly as a man could be, with wens on his face and eyes as black as sin. His face was in shadow and flickering light from the torch that multiplied his hideousness. But I had seen him practice combat back in the yard at Duffield Castle before William had thrown us out and I recalled his speed and viciousness.

The mace in Walter's other hand glistened and had pieces of skin and hair stuck to the flanges.

Shouts echoed and the screaming began again but this time it did not stop. It did come from the hall, beyond Walter. There was the clashing and ringing of weapons now. My men fighting the attackers.

If Walter was in my house then that meant William was too.

"That's right, boy," Walter laughed at the expression on

my face. "He has come for you." Walter stood his ground blocking my way to the hall. "Fall to your knees now and welcome your fate. Come, Richard, come and feed the Angel of the Lord. Offer up your blood. Offer up the blood of your wife and children."

I leapt forward in a headlong charge but he was expecting to provoke me so I checked my forward motion and ducked under his mace. Fighting had always been easy for me but Walter was faster than any man I had faced. Only by the grace of God did the weapon skim through my hair to smash through the wall plaster above my head.

My sword flicked up into his face but he was so fast. He weaved sideways, dropped his mace and stepped forward while drawing a knife that he slashed low toward my guts and balls. But I was fast, too. And I was unencumbered, young and filled with hatred and vengeance. I twisted from his lunge, stepping sideways to smash my blade into his forearm shattering his bones through the mail. His weight carried him forward while I stepped beyond him. I reversed my sword and ran him through at the base of the spine. I forced my blade through his mail coat so hard the point ran deep into the plaster and pinned him face forward to the wall.

Swooping up his dagger I held the point against his neck under the ear.

"How many are you?" I said, breathing hard. "Are my horses guarded?"

From the cries coming through the walls, my fighting men sounded desperate. I had merely four and one was a boy and one an old man and I knew that they could do nothing more than delay William's men who were brutal, experienced warriors.

"He has come for you," Walter said. "Earl William will feast upon your flesh. You are the cup and he shall drink of you."

"My horses," I said, hissing in his ear. "How many men guard my stable?"

Walter laughed. "We shall cover the earth with our numbers. You will become one of us or you shall feed us. And you shall eat the flesh of your sons and the flesh of your daughters. And all shall eat the flesh of their neighbours. For he is the Destroyer, the Angel of the—"

I punched the dagger into the base of his skull – a quicker death than he deserved – and pulled my sword out. Walter collapsed, his dead eyes staring at the Hell that awaited him.

William had come. No doubt there were men in my stable. Unless William had left such a menial task for Hugo the Giant or a gifted swordsman like Roger of Tyre then I would be able to take our horses.

But would I have time to saddle two of them and would Alice and I be able to outrun William's men all the way back to Jaffa? We would have a child each on our horse and it was a long ride. Our horses would tire or die if we rode hard all the way. And galloping through the moonlight could cause a horse to trip and even a single fall would mean death. I imagined sending Alice with Emma and Jocelyn on his pony off while I kept William's men fighting but they could have run her down easily while keeping me from leaving.

Perhaps I should have gone back to our room to say farewell to Alice and the children. We could have spent our last few moments together instead of leaving them alone and waiting for a man who would never come.

There seemed to be only one course of action. So I went toward the sound of the screaming with my sword at the ready, fantasising that I might finally have my vengeance.

My hall was where we ate, as a household, and where some of the servants slept. It was where I spoke to my tenants and it was rather finely decorated, though Alice assured me it was terribly old-fashioned. It was the beating heart of our home and our estate and it was an almost sacred space.

I found it full of blood and death. Because of the clashing weapons and shouts and screams I expected to find my four men valiantly facing off against William's knights.

Instead, the fighting was over. Two of my men had been cut into bloody pieces and scattered about the floor, blood soaking into the rushes. The other two men were panting and bleeding from head wounds surrounded by half a dozen of William's armoured men who were prodding and jeering at them. I did not recognise William's new men. They were all were in hauberks or the shorter haubergeons and carrying swords, daggers, falchions and axes and a spear.

It was like watching bear baiting. My men were barely defending themselves, resigned to their fate. They were already bleeding to death so they had every right to be. The clanging of weapons was no doubt to encourage me to come running.

Eight of my servants lay bound and beaten on the floor at the centre of the hall by the cold hearth. Ralph the Reaper was torturing them by slashing the soles of their feet into bloody ribbons. The cook and his girl had been murdered. The others were groaning and screaming in pain and terror.

And there was William.

Standing at the head of my hall as if he owned it, leaning against my table. He was in a half-rusted hauberk and helmet. The surcoat covering his mail was of fine cloth dyed red though it was filthy and stained all over with the brown mottled pattern of old blood. His face lit up with a smile when he saw me.

"I told you he would come," William cried, clapping his hands together. "What a fine knight you are, Richard, to come save these worthless peasants rather than finish swyving your whore." He laughed heartily, looking down at my nakedness. His men, too, laughed and stood staring at me, no longer tormenting my own.

All together there were eight of William's men. Ralph the Reaper standing over my servants, the six armed and armoured men tormenting my men and William himself standing tall and terrible at the far end beyond his men.

My two men leaned upon each other breathing heavily. Neither could provide me with help in a fight. The servants would be worse than useless. Those that were not tied up in the hall were probably already dead.

I regretted not riding hard for Jaffa with Alice. Perhaps there was yet time, I thought, and edged backward toward the corridor.

"You cannot run," William said, as if he was disappointed in me. He stalked forward with his sword still sheathed at his hip. "My men have your horses. They are praying for you to make an attempt for them."

I wanted to scream in frustration. "There is no need for you to do this," I said.

William stopped, his face a mask of pretended shock. "No need? Need? What need have you to ask after me through all the towns and cities of Outremer? Well, seek me no longer for here I am." He flung his arms wide. "So, you want to kill me, Richard?"

"I seek you no longer," I said and he scoffed. Some of his men chuckled. "You murdered my brother and his family. And so many others. I swore to bring you to justice. But I gave up my search. I would never have bothered you again."

"Truly?" William asked, as if he was surprised. "But why would you give up your duty to your dear brother?" He spat out the last word as if the taste of it were repulsive.

I did not want to speak to William of my happiness. "I gave up," I said.

"Ah," William said, nodding to his men as if everything made sense now. "So you are suggesting that I allow you to live because you are incompetent? Or because you are lazy?" His men laughed. Ralph the Reaper cackled like a madman.

"Leave us in peace," I hefted the war sword in my right hand and Walter's dagger in my left. "Save yourself the trouble."

"But trouble is what we are here for, brother," William said and laughed. Again, his men laughed with him. He sighed. "I hoped for a long time that you and I could become friends."

William nodded at his six men. They hacked my men down with brutal efficiency. Neither men had time to utter a sound before they were dead. William's new soldiers spread out away from the bodies. They encircled me to cut me off from the corridor behind.

I recalled Henry's body, beheaded, dismembered. His torso laying upon a jumble of shit-stinking guts trailing from a great black wound slashed from hip to hip.

The men were grim. Their eyes had the dead gaze of those that who have seen too much of war.

Doing the unexpected in a fight can often keep you alive. Nevertheless, when I darted forward, stark naked, into the centre of those six battle-hardened, armoured men I knew I was charging to my death.

Speed was the single advantage I had. Or so I thought.

William bellowed a warning but by then I was already upon the two men in the centre of the curving line of six. The one on the right held a spear that I could get inside the reach of. He had time enough to raise it and step back once before I was beyond the head of it and I stabbed the point of my sword through the bridge of his nose. He fell back, screaming and dying, his spear flung away clattering on the floor and my blade was already out and moving, my feet carrying me away from the attack I sensed coming.

The man next to the spearman swung his mace back handed, round in an arc and upwards to smash the side of my jaw but I leaned down so it whooshed over my ear and I stabbed my long blade through his unarmoured knee. Crunching through the joint, my blade scraped on the edges of the bones. I moved forward to finish him but the others were closing so I danced back out of the way.

From nowhere, Ralph the Reaper was there at my elbow and he slashed overarm with a wicked curved dagger. By God, he was fast. Too fast for me to even flinch and it sliced deep into my skin along my bare upper arm before I could pull away. I snarled and lunged at him. For I was fast, too, and in his panic to retreat he tripped over the bound servants underfoot. Ralph fell amongst them and I kicked the knife over in desperate hope any servant could free themselves and skipped away across the room from the other knights moving up behind me.

Too late I realised how they had herded me away from the hall entrance. I watched aghast as William slipped into the corridor that lead to my bed chamber.

He was going for Alice.

I moved to chase him but those men moved like cats pouncing and they cut me off, weapons up.

"Alice!" I bellowed. "Alice, run!"

The one chance I had was to cut through them but when

I charged forward they backed away leaving two men covering the corridor doorway, where William had gone. There was no way through. When I advanced on them I exposed my back to the others and spun to deflect the blows aimed at my back. Every man there was faster than they had a right to be. I barely got back into the hall without being gutted.

Ralph the Reaper regained his feet and joined them so there were five around me plus the man wounded in the knee who stayed down, groaning and bleeding near the servants who were crawling back out of the way leaving trails of blood from their slashed feet.

I had to save Alice.

I barrelled toward the one with an axe and as he scurried back he stumbled on the severed arm of one of my men and fell. I was on him and slashed down on his helmet so hard it bent the steel and I stomped my heel down on his face hard, hoping he would choke on his teeth. The bones of his face cut my foot open but I hardly felt it as I ducked away from the others and swung my blade at one who came too close. I was surprised to feel the edge of my blade crush that man's throat and he went down without uttering a noise and suffocated, his heels drumming upon the floor.

Three, now. Three men who waited calmly for me to come to them. Two stood between me and Alice and they knew all they had to do was keep me in the hall rather than fight me. Ralph the Reaper stood to one side, grinning.

Alice screamed. It was a cry of anguish and anger and it was the worst sound I ever heard.

I charged forward for the doorway. The two in front closed in on me and I checked my dash, meaning to duck to one side and force one man into the other to get around them.

But the blood welling from my wounded heel caused my foot to slip and my leading leg slid forward. A deep-down reflex caused me to throw my arms out wide to keep my balance and I watched in surprise as one of the men ran me through with his sword.

It was like being punched in the stomach but I watched the point of the sword snick through the skin of my stomach and I could not stop myself from moving forward and down and it kept on pushing through until the cross guard slammed into my body.

Even back then when I was young, I had seen a great number of men killed. They often wore the same expression. One of shock and disbelief. As though every man was thinking the same thought in the moment he received a mortal wound. *This cannot be happening to me.* The fact that I was naked and could see precisely how the blade pushed the skin deep into the wound made the fact of my death inescapable. Yet I have no doubt I was wearing that very same expression when the man who had run his sword through my belly butted his helm into my face and the blow crushed my nose and knocked me out.

A wound of such severity as impalement by a thirty-inch sword is a significant shock for the body. But was nothing to what I felt when I was slapped awake.

Two of William's men held me upright, while Ralph the Reaper stood to one side held a dagger to my throat. My blood was flowing from my wound to soak my stomach, loins and legs in shining dark blood.

Before me, both facing me; William stood behind Alice, towering over her. He held her upright with mailed fists digging tight into the bare flesh of her upper arms.

The children lay sobbing on the floor next to her, both had been struck and Jocelyn had been beaten bloody. Both were scarcely conscious. The boy, especially seemed badly hurt.

Alice's eyes were filled with tears and hatred. Hatred for William and the men in her hall. And, I am sure, hatred for me for bringing them down upon her and her children.

"You cannot die yet, Richard," William cried as I blinked away tears. "You must witness me feast upon your wife. For the Lord God has commanded me to eat the flesh of a thousand women. And He has commanded me to eat the flesh of their sons and the flesh of their daughters. And when the time is come, all men shall eat the flesh of their neighbours and devote to destruction all that they have. Do not spare them, He has commanded, but kill both man and woman, child and infant, ox and sheep, camel and donkey. You mortals shall present your bodies to me as living sacrifice. The old has passed away. Behold, the new has come. I am the resurrection and the life. Whomsoever feeds me with their flesh, though he die, yet shall he live in me, and everyone who lives and feeds me shall never die but help me grow stronger with every feast of living flesh from this day until the coming end of days."

He bared his teeth like a rabid dog and threw down his jaws upon Alice's neck. She screamed and writhed but William's fingers dug into her and blood welled from her throat and flowed down her shift. Emma screamed and buried her face against her brother's chest.

The men holding me had the kind of strength that only seasoned warriors can ever obtain. An iron steadiness that comes after years of holding up a shield and swinging a sword every day while wearing heavy armour. I had lost pints of blood and more pumped steadily from my guts. My face was mangled so much I struggled to draw breath.

But rage filled my arms with strength.

I roared and grabbed the men who held me and heaved

backwards and down, leaning back from Ralph's dagger and rowing backward with my arms to drag them down off their feet with me. Their animal instinct took over and they released my arms to brace their fall. The pain of hitting the floor took my breath away but they were caught off guard and were wearing armour so fell heavier than I did.

The man on my right twisted away and fell out of reach but the one of the left was laying half under me. I reached across his body and drew the sword from his scabbard. In the same motion I swung it back hand over and down into the other man's face so the edge cracked through his skull across the eye sockets, crushing his eyes and face into pulp. I dropped the sword, rolled over and pulled that man's dagger from his waist and rolled back to thrust it into the other man's temple. It ground against bone and my hands were too weak and slippery with blood to free the blade.

As I struggled, Ralph the Reaper leapt on top of me, straddling my hips, laughing like a maniac. He stabbed me once, twice and a third time in the chest before I could grab the back of his head with one hand and punch my thumb into his eyeball, bursting it.

He screamed and dropped his dagger to hold his destroyed eye socket. I grabbed his dagger and hacked into the veins of his neck, drenching me with hot blood as he flopped onto me in panic, not realising that he was already dead. The blood gushing from his neck spewed into my face and into my mouth and I could not avoid swallowing many mouthfuls of his blood before I pushed his body off me. I felt the hot liquid sliding down my throat and the warmth of it churned in my stomach. I wiped it from my eyes.

It was not until later that I discovered that ingesting human blood heals my body. Perhaps it was Ralph's blood that gave me the strength to stand after being stabbed repeatedly in the lungs. But all I knew was that instead of dying I was able to climb to my feet.

Alice still held upright by William but was drenched with her own blood and her head was flopped forward. Her hair hung wet with blood in ribbons over her face. She seemed dead.

William looked up, his face dripping with my wife's blood. His eyes were wide and he dropped Alice to the ground. She fell heavily and her head cracked into the floor by her children. She lay still.

William backed away from her, drawing his sword.

"How is it that you yet stand?" William's voice sounded far away. He gestured at my chest, my guts. "You should be dead."

I took a step toward him. "Not until..." I started to say until blood welled up from my lungs and choked me. I could not take a breath. My head swam and I fell to one knee but I forced myself to my feet.

William lowered the point of his sword, his head tilted to one side as he regarded me.

I lunged forward, waving my dagger at him.

William scoffed and backed away to the door.

"I think that you will die," William said to me, hesitantly.

My vision blurred and I dropped to one knee, leaning on it. My head dropped and I could see the state of my chest and gut, with blood weeping from my body. The chest wounds bubbled and sucked with air. It was not possible that I lived.

Two men came into the hall from outside and William spoke to them but I was dying and my sight and hearing were failing. One of the men I am sure was Hugo the Giant. They stooped to the floor and carried things away with them.

I hauled myself upright and opened my mouth to curse him but blood ran from my lips and I coughed and fought for breath. It was as though my chest had iron bands around it.

William laughed and stepped backwards into the doorway that lead outside into the night. Was he afraid of me?

I sank to one knee again. William was just a streak of

colour in my blurring vision. The darkness crept inward from the outside.

"I will not desecrate your corpse," William's shape said to me before he vanished. "I will leave some of your servants to bury you. I owe you that much."

I inched across the floor to my wife. Alice was dead. Her eyes stared up, empty of life yet filled with accusation.

Jocelyn and Emma were gone. William had taken her children.

I drowned in blood.

CHAPTER SEVEN
REBIRTH

I AWOKE TO SCREAMS AND CONFUSED FACES.
Then I slept and woke and slept.

Light speared through the shuttered windows across my
bed and onto the blankets that covered me. Alice was not
next to me and then I remembered and I despaired.

Servants clattered and banged in the house and out in
the stables. Someone was sawing wood. There was the
regular thwack of a pick digging into the hard earth.

I slid from my bed and stood. Someone had dressed me

in a clean, long loose shirt. I pulled it off to inspect my wounds.

My body was healed. There was not a scratch upon the skin of my chest or my stomach. Not even a scar.

In fact, I felt strong, fast, and more alert than I ever had before.

Opening the shutters, the sun bathed me in heat. It felt glorious. My skin was alive with the light and the warm wind blew upon my face.

It was all so strange that I held on to a faint hope that it had all been a nightmare. Pulling on my shirt I walked to my hall.

In the corridor there was the damage to the wall from my duel with Walter and a huge blood stain. When I walked into the hall itself my servants stopped washing the floor and came toward me and fell to their knees.

It had not been a nightmare.

For a time I kept to my bed and drank wine. Someone sent a physician from Jaffa and I had to growl and threaten to stop him from examining my body. Because he did not know what else to do he looked closely at my urine. I would not let him bleed me.

A few days later the King himself came to visit me.

"The physician tells me that you died," Richard of England said, standing over my bed, his fair hair filled with golden light from the window.

"That tells you everything you need to know about physicians."

That made him laugh. "God save us from the pissprophets. They will be the death of us all. Still, you were pierced through the chest many times. Your servants were actually burying you when you took a breath. Scared the life right out of the poor bastards." He laughed again. He was nervous.

"So I heard," I said.

The survivors of the attack had told me and everyone else what a miracle my survival was. The ones who had been tied up in the hall had seen me kill most of the enemy. In their eyes I had driven William and the rest away.

My grave had already been dug, set apart from the graves of my servants as was proper, when I sat up.

"God must have plans for you on earth," King Richard said, with the confidence of a man who had been so honoured since the moment that his father's seed had quickened in his mother's womb.

"Perhaps He did not want me in Heaven," I said, morose and unappreciative that the most lauded king of Christendom had taken the time to travel to my estate and was being kind and generous to me. His guards lurked in the background and I could feel their silent displeasure radiating across the room.

"Come with me to England," Richard said, sitting upon the bed next to my legs. "My dear little brother is being rather troublesome and I need good men with me to put things right." His eyes took on a faraway look. "In truth, there is trouble in many of my lands. Plenty of work for a man of your abilities. And evident gifts."

"Why would you want me?" I said, ungraciously.

Richard was not a man to be trifled with and for a moment I saw his face cloud with anger. But then he smiled.

"There is no man I would rather have by my side in battle," Richard the Lionheart said to me. This remains one of the finest compliments I ever had.

"And besides," he leaned over and punched a fist into my shoulder as if making a joke. "You recover from wounds that would kill a bull. Perhaps you can teach me your secret." He coughed to cover his embarrassment at his clumsy joke but of course he was intrigued by my recovery.

"I have a task, my lord," I said, embarrassed by his affection. "One I should have completed long ago."

He shrugged. "I have left instructions for Henry. I am certain that you heard how my nephew Henry has married the queen of Jerusalem. That means he is now the king and the most powerful Christian in the Holy Land. Once I am gone. Henry will provide you with guides and men. After all, it is in their interest to round up such a villain. You shall finally bring William de Ferrers to justice. I simply regret I shall not be able to witness his punishment."

"I am honoured by your confidence in me, my lord." The king still did not understand the depths of William's evil.

When you are done, you will join me in England then I shall find you a new... a suitable estate. You could hold William's lands. It should probably be yours anyway, I am sure and perhaps I could make it official. What would you say to that, Richard? Duffield Castle and all the rest."

I had an inkling that Richard was one of those men who would promise things he did not mean, especially to strong young men he held in high esteem. There were always rumours that he was a secret sodomite. And perhaps he was but he seemed to me to simply be full of passion, not lust. His enthusiasm consumed him and he esteemed soldiers very highly indeed, so long as they were useful.

Perhaps he truly did believe I knew how to cheat death. Either way, there was no chance he would pass over greater lords to grant the likes of me such a vast estate.

"Thank you, my lord," I said. "That is very generous of you."

"With the invincible Richard of Ashbury at my side, I shall conquer all who stand against me, shall I not?"

Everything that man said was spoken with such absolute confidence that I could never be sure when he was speaking with sincerity or in jest.

"You shall, lord." I muttered.

He left for England the next day.

I never saw him again.

While I was lying dead myself I had missed Alice's burial. She had been taken to a family crypt in Jaffa. Her cousins told my servants in no uncertain terms that my body could be tossed down a well in the desert for all they cared. And thank God her family were ungenerous bastards or I might have woken in a coffin, inside a lead box locked in a crypt. Her family in Jaffa shut their doors to me. As well as losing Alice they had lost Jocelyn, who could have become a lord. And they had lost sweet little Emma who would have made a good marriage to further the family's wealth and renown.

After setting my house in order, I rode to Acre to meet with Henry de Champagne. A king by marriage only, he never referred to himself as King of Jerusalem in part because we had lost the city after Hattin.

The king, Richard had told me, would help me hunt William. He would put all the power of Outremer at my disposal. I knew I would need gold and silver for bribes to discover where he was hiding and guides to take me there. And I would need at least a dozen good knights with horses and remounts, fully equipped and supplied.

∞

"I cannot provide you with men," Henry of Champagne said over his shoulder while his armourer measured his limbs with string.

We were at his palace in Acre. It was still a new home for him so his knights and attendants were everywhere on hand to ensure he made it his own. The palace was beautiful but I had been shown through up to the top of it where the king had his apartments. The queen was nowhere to be seen and she was rarely spoken of. Once, she had been powerful and beautiful. But I am sure that for Henry she was nothing more than a tool to make him king.

Henry stood in the good light pouring in from the huge open sides of the room, most of which opened onto balconies and so the sea wind could flow in from three sides of the room and keep the royal person cool while in the city below the people roasted and gasped in the airless streets. Beyond the windows the sea was so blue it hurt my eyes.

A long table ran the length of the wall, covered in the armourer's measuring tools and many examples of his fine work. Next to me lay rows of helmets polished to such a gleam that I could see my distorted reflection in them.

It was an informal audience. That meant I had been forced to wait for days in the city before Henry allowed me inside, then made me wait all morning on a bench outside his chambers and then when I was hurried inside he hardly acknowledged my existence.

No doubt he felt duty bound to see me, as his uncle had insisted. Henry owed his kingly position entirely to Richard's political manoeuvring and, so rumour said, a paid assassination. But our joint benefactor had sailed for Europe and Henry was too busy picking out his new royal armour to bother overly much with me.

"I understand, my lord," I said. What else could I say? He was my liege lord.

"Well, I'm not giving you money, either," he muttered. He was not much older than me but he was a big, burly man and filled with royal authority. "How much longer will this take?" This was directed at the arthritic armourer who was mumbling measurements to his assistants.

"Almost done, my lord king, but perfection takes time, you understand. Your armour will be impenetrable only so long as the fit is perfection itself. No weapon shall harm you, I swear it. You shall be invulnerable upon the battlefield, impervious to blade or—"

"Yes, yes, just get on with it," Henry said, then glanced over his shoulder at me again. "So if you do not want men or money, what in God's name do you want?"

In fact, I did want men and money and had fully expected plenty of both. I resisted the urge to shove King Henry out of his God damned window.

"Information, my lord," I said, resigning myself to lower expectations. "Introduction to men who know lands where William is rumoured to be hiding. Having spoken to many people while I awaited this audience, I suspect he is hiding beyond Outremer. Possibly in an abandoned fortress somewhere in the desert. If that is in fact where he is I shall also need to approach the Saracens who control the land near there. You, my lord king, could perhaps request peaceful passage through those lands."

"Yes, yes, of course he is. It sounds like a lot of bother to go through, does it not?" Henry said, without looking me in the eye. "I think we should let the Saracens kill him. We know that he's gone to ground half way to Damascus. He won't last long up there with those heathens roaming about. He will be dead before the year is out, mark my words. Probably best to forget about William and be on your way."

I fought down my urge to grab one of the helmets from the table and smash his idiot face in. I kept my voice level. "Are you saying that you know that is where William is?"

He hesitated then wafted away my question. "I am saying that you need take no action for William to be killed. He shall not live to see Christmas, I have no doubt."

"I must perform the task with my own hand," I said, stiffly. "I swore an oath, my lord. It must be fulfilled."

"Yes, yes, your famous oath. Is there anyone in Outremer who has not heard of it? Dear me, what a chivalrous man you are."

I ground my teeth, lest I sink them into his face.

At least he had the good grace to appear embarrassed when he turned around and saw the look in my eyes. Embarrassed or fearful, perhaps. "That is to say, I heard what he did to your wife, of course. A terrible thing. An unholy thing. I had the honour of meeting her merely twice but she struck me as a remarkable lady."

"She was, my lord."

"Still, she's in a better place now, I don't doubt," Henry muttered.

I looked out to sea while the armourer finished his measuring and bowed and made further promises that Henry waved away.

A servant brought Henry wine and the king walked to the open window that looked out to that brilliant blue sea beyond. Wine was not offered to me.

"I wish I could help you," Henry said without looking at me. "But if I send my knights into Saladin's lands so soon after the peace treaty is signed then I could start another war."

"I have no quarrel with any Saracen," I said.

Henry glanced over at me and chuckled. "Do not let God hear you say such a thing."

"I fought to regain the Kingdom of Jerusalem, sire," I said. I was willing to act humble if it meant getting what I needed. "I would never do anything to endanger the peace. But the treaty does allow travel by pilgrims and traders, does it not? I would pretend to be a merchant looking to buy spices, perhaps."

He turned and leaned on the railing that ran across the window. It creaked under his weight.

"You do not have the disposition required for deceit," he said. "And you could never pass for a merchant."

I did not know whether to be offended or feel complimented so I said nothing.

"So," the king said. "Tell me truthfully. If I tell you that I will not only provide you with no support but that I expressly forbid you to travel into Saracen land, what would you do?"

I took a deep breath and said nothing.

"You would go anyway," Henry said. "You would disobey your king for the sake of your oath."

It was pointless to object.

"So you leave me with a decision to make, Richard,"

Henry said, talking down to me as if he had gained wisdom along with his kingdom, though he and I were of an age. "Should I throw you in gaol now, before you can start a war?"

He watched my face carefully for a reaction. "I would pray that you not do so, my lord," I managed to say.

"If I took such an action against most of my knights then his family and friends would pressure me to release him. After all, you have committed no crime. But you, I am sad to say, have no friends or family."

He was goading me but I did not know why. "I have friends," I said.

Henry sighed. "You are a difficult man to know, Richard. I think most men are afraid of you."

"Of me?" I was shocked.

"Many of us have seen you fight," Henry said. "And some men are afraid that you will be like William."

"What in God's name do you mean? Why would any man think that?"

Henry looked alarmed and held up his hands. "Of course I know you are a decent man. But you make others nervous."

"What is your point?" I said. "My lord."

Henry let out a breath and leaned on the window railing again. "If I was a ruthless king then I would lock you up until William gets himself killed." He left the words hanging between us before continuing. "I wonder what dear Uncle Richard would do in my position."

I reckoned that if he thought it would serve his interests Richard would have me quietly killed. "He would give me men and pray God grant strength to my arm, my lord."

Henry looked uncomfortable and he hesitated for a long while. "The Archbishop of Tyre has an Egyptian priest. This Egyptian has been in the city for some days now. He claims to know where William is hiding."

It took a moment for me to respond. "Why not tell me this immediately?" I said, my irritation no doubt apparent for he threw me a warning look. "My lord." I was ready to walk out and find the priest myself.

But Henry smiled and turned back to the view. Ships bobbed in the harbour, bringing wealth from everywhere in the world into Henry's kingdom. No wonder he could not stop looking at it.

"I have no way of knowing this Egyptian's true intent," he said. "Perhaps he is telling the truth and William is preying upon locals and travellers but if that is so, why do the Saracens not clear William out of his refuge?"

"What does this Egyptian priest say to that?"

"He says that Saladin wants the Franks to deal with the Frankish demon," Henry scoffed. "The Archbishop tells me he pressed the old man and he admitted that the Saracens are wary of him. Can you credit such a thing, Richard? Saladin afraid of William de Ferrers and a handful of outlawed knights and bandits? Absurd."

I could well believe it so I said nothing.

Henry held out his cup for more wine. "But what if Saladin is baiting a trap for us? Perhaps, Saladin has been waiting for King Richard to sail home and now he wishes to provoke me into sending my knights into Saracen lands and so breach the peace."

"But if you send me out there with just a man or two then you could always deny you had knowledge of my actions," I said.

Henry drank his wine. "If you are captured by the enemy in such circumstances I would be unable to pay your ransom."

I actually laughed, surprising everyone in the room including myself. "I do not expect I will be held for ransom, my lord."

"I suppose not," he allowed. "Draw up a letter for the Archbishop," Henry said to one of his servants. "Hand the Egyptian priest over to Richard of Ashbury and send them on their way into Palestine. Have the Archbishop pay for their supplies and horses and so on. And draw up a letter from me instructing Richard here to escort the priest back to Damascus. Make it very short and have the Latin translated into Arabic and added underneath. That way, Richard, if you are captured it looks better for me and for the kingdom."

"I understand. And thank you, my lord," I said and I meant it.

"I pray God gives strength to your arm," Henry the King of Jerusalem said. "Truly, Richard. I will pray for you."

∞

"An unholy mess," the Archbishop of Tyre said to me as he led me through his palace in Acre. One of his men escorted us. "Your Earl William has put us in rather a difficult situation."

The Archbishop had the Coptic priest locked away in a room on the third floor of the tower of the Archbishop's Palace and I walked through those cool corridors and up the stairs. There were old, cracked pictures painted upon many of the walls that showed many figures frozen in action that must have once been brightly coloured but had now faded.

"Yes, Archbishop," I replied, not sure what he wanted me to say.

"Preying upon honest pilgrims and travellers," the

Archbishop said. "Something must be done."

He was an old man and he was not tall or broad and yet he possessed a great moral authority and he walked briskly. He had been the Archbishop for a long time. I knew his name was Joscius but no one would have ever called him anything other than Archbishop.

"Yes, Archbishop."

"I would rather not be involved in this," he said to me, conspiratorially. "But I feel a certain responsibility for the situation."

I could not imagine why he would feel such a thing. "Yes, Archbishop."

"So it would be a welcome relief if you could help us. I would be rid of this priest," the Archbishop explained. "And you can take him off my hands."

"I will take him as my guide with a glad heart," I said. "But if you have wanted to rid of him, my lord Archbishop, why have you kept him locked up?"

"I told you why," the Archbishop said, his voice flailing me. "Something must done about Earl William."

"William must die," I said, nodding.

The Archbishop sighed. "I wish it were not so." He stopped outside a heavy door. "But I fear you are correct," he said, peering up at me. "In here."

He invited me to peer through the viewing slot. It was

not a gaol cell but a comfortable room. There was a bed and a table and a high, slit window showing a streak of brilliant blue. The priest lay upon the bed, evidently sleeping and shrouded in a sheet.

"You tortured him?" I asked the Archbishop before we went in.

He frowned. "Of course not. We simply asked him some questions."

"You trust his answers?"

The Archbishop sighed. "My men have made enquiries. He is known in these parts. They tell me that for a long time he was a hermit in the Sinai and a few years ago he left the desert and travelled through Outremer, administering to the local Christians. His touch was said to be holy and he lived on charity. He tells me he has been in Damascus, living happily enough under the Saracens and seeing to the poor Christian souls there. Did you know there are thousands of them there? My men found someone who knew him and brought the fellow here. He confirmed this was Antonius of the Sinai."

"So, forgive me, Archbishop but why lock him up?"

The Archbishop gave me a long look. "Perhaps the desert addled his brains. He certainly looks as shrivelled as a dried date. But he argues with himself when alone."

I shrugged. "Just because he is mad, does not mean he is

a liar."

"Indeed not. But I am uncertain of his trustworthiness. And you should be too. Shall we go in?"

It was fairly clean. Even the nightsoil bucket was empty.

"My Lord Archbishop," the little old man said as he sat up. He had very dark skin, wrinkled and tough and shiny like the bark of an ancient tree. When his startlingly blue eyes flicked over my face I saw a glint of surprise in them.

"Antonius, this is Richard of Ashbury," the Archbishop said. "He has come to ask you some questions."

"More questions? Why do you Franks always have so many questions?" Antonius asked, his French heavily accented but otherwise faultless.

"Where is William?" I asked.

"I told the Archbishop's men," he said, looking to the Archbishop. The Archbishop said nothing and shuffled away toward the narrow window. "But I would very much enjoy telling you all over again."

"So where is he?"

"The hills of Golan," the priest said. "North of the Sea of Galilee."

"Where exactly?" I said.

He looked surprised. "I do not know where they are hiding. No one knows. The Saracens know simply the rough area where men disappear."

"Why do the Saracens not hunt him down? Their access to Jaffa from Damascus is almost cut off by William's raids on the merchants. Surely they want to end him? They certainly have the means."

Antonius shrugged his little sparrow shoulders. "They sent men. But the demons melt into the hills and cannot be found. And also, Lord William is a Christian baron of Tripoli. Perhaps if the Saracens were to kill him, your king Henry would see this as a betrayal of the treaty and use it as an excuse to start a war? Perhaps, some in Damascus say, the Baron William is there with the support of the king?"

The Archbishop spun around. "That is a lie. We do not condone this monster's actions. We want peace. We want trade and we want pilgrimage to Jerusalem. William is an outlaw."

The little priest spread his hands. "It is not I that says this. I tell you merely why perhaps Saladin does not wish to solve the Frank's problem."

"You are willing to lead me to the area?" I asked him.

Antonius shrugged. "Very well. Perhaps I shall take you to where they were last seen. But then I shall continue home upon the Damascus road."

"I will let you go when I find William," I said to Antonius. "If we do not find him then I shall bring you back here."

The priest opened his mouth to argue, looked between me and the Archbishop and closed his mouth. It was curious that he did not object further to such unreasonable treatment.

The Archbishop looked at me.

"He'll do," I said.

"Come," the Archbishop said and we left the priest's cell, leaving him sitting on the bed with his skinny legs dangling off the edge like some ancient child. "You shall be released into this man's custody soon. I suggest you spend the time praying."

The Archbishop's man slammed and locked the door behind us.

"What do you think?" the Archbishop asked me in the corridor.

"I do not know," I said.

The Archbishop nodded. "Good."

I do not trust you either, I thought. "If he can bring me near to William then that will do well enough," I said. "King Henry said you would give me men," I said to the Archbishop.

"He did, did he?" The Archbishop said. "Well, I suppose you can take Adelard, here." He gestured to his man, who looked surprised and then silently furious, his face colouring and his jaw tensing.

"Thank you, my lord Archbishop. The king said I could take four men," I lied.

The Archbishop scowled. "Adelard, who is your best man?"

Adelard, an older man who looked sturdy and steady but angry, cleared his throat. "Young Elias."

The Archbishop nodded. "You can have my two best men and you will be grateful for that much."

"I am, my lord Archbishop," I said, thinking about some of the taverns where I could hire more men.

I thought I would be escorted out yet the Archbishop hesitated. "You may wonder why I take such an interest in this situation," he said.

"Because God wants peace?" I said.

A flicker of irritation passed over his face and he walked back the way we had arrived, his heels echoing down corridor. Me and his man Adelard hurried to catch up and he continued. "After the Battle of Hattin, Earl William came to see me. He felt he had experienced a profound revelation."

"You knew William?" I was shocked.

He ignored me as he stepped into the spiral tower steps and instead of going down the way we had come, he went up and I followed, wondering what in God's name the Archbishop had to tell me about William.

"Let us converse in here," he gestured me into a lavish room near the top of the tower. The room opened to a balcony on one side with views out across the compact city and the sea beyond. There was a silver cross on the wall and a large golden cross with jewels embedded upon a table by one wall and decorated in an ornate, almost Saracen style with colourful and richly patterned carpets and cushions. I took the seat he invited me to take; a delicate chair carved with curving olive leaves near the balcony and watched him ease his old bones into a huge, gold leafed thing like a throne opposite me. He let out a huge sigh, wincing a little and when he was settled he closed his eyes for a moment and I wondered if he was going to fall asleep.

"So you knew William, my lord?" I asked.

His eyes snapped open and he sighed again. "Speaking about these things brings me no joy. But there are things you must know."

A servant brought a jug of cold, sweet lemon water that he poured into silver cups. The Archbishop took a long drink and smacked his thin lips.

"Five years ago the largest Christian army ever assembled in this kingdom rode out from Jerusalem to meet Saladin. Foolish. Impetuous. I knew it would end in disaster but what warrior listens to an ancient, decrepit priest like me? Thousands of knights rode out from all over Outremer, with tens of thousands of soldiers in their wake, so certain that they would smash the Saracens. They were impressive as they marched off. Well, they all died. Thousands upon thousands of them slaughtered in the dust and the fools left Jerusalem emptied of men able to protect the Holy City. Those poor souls who could not escape Jerusalem, thousands of them, sold into slavery."

He shook his head. He had tears welling in his eyes. I stifled a sigh and settled into my seat.

"Then Jaffa and Acre fell and everything collapsed. We fell back from city after city. Those idiots threw away the Holy Land. Only thanks to King Richard of England have we regained some of what was lost."

"Yes, Archbishop," I said. "All Christendom has been awash with the tales."

His head snapped up. "The young are ever impatient. You rush toward death, never taking the time to appreciate where you are." He indicated the room around us and then the sea beyond the balcony.

I leaned forward. "I swore an oath to God to kill William. You want me to take that priest from you and kill William. If you have something to tell me about William that will help me do my duty to God, please do so, my lord Archbishop."

The servant poured the old man another cup of the

lemon water while he regarded me with a look I could not read. "Did you know William's wife and son were killed?"

"William was married?" It took a moment for my mind to adjust. "I never knew he took a wife. And he had a son?"

"A babe in arms. They were murdered, in the madness that followed after Hattin." He looked at me strangely, carefully, judging my reaction.

"But I thought Saladin enslaved the Christians of Jerusalem. Not killed them."

The Archbishop nodded. "It was not the Saracens but Frankish knights who murdered them." He sighed. "It was a very bad time. There was no law. The survivors of the battle fled in front of the Saracens as fast as their stolen horses could carry them. Homes were looted and people were killed."

"William survived the attack?"

"William was laying among the dead at Hattin when it happened. He knew nothing of the murder when he came to me, back from the dead, filthy and stinking but filled with the light of the Lord."

"I have suspected that his madness began at Hattin."

The Archbishop shook his head. "He was struck down in the battle and thrown into a mound of Christian dead. William lay in that mountain of death for two days, dying. He told me he had a vision of God. There was a bright light, warm and peaceful but instead of welcoming William into Heaven God told him to drink. God told him to become the cup of Christ. So William drank the foul blood that was leaking down onto him from the men above and around him. And that blood gave him strength enough to push his way out and rise up to fight his way clear, killing forty Saracens and stealing a horse and returning to me ahead of Saladin's forces."

"Forty Saracens? I wonder that you did not lock him in a dungeon for such ravings."

"It was a miracle. I told him as much." The Archbishop looked up at the ceiling. "You must understand that he seemed far from mad. He was filled with God, I tell you. Any man could have seen he was filled with joy, not madness. There was such vitality to him, such vigour and clarity. In the face of that terrible defeat I took it as a sign from God that there was yet hope. That the Christian kingdoms in the Holy Land would likewise return from the dead to take back what we lost."

"He has used that vigour to murder uncounted innocents."

"It was when he returned home to find his wife violated and murdered and infant son slain that he lost his mind. Can you imagine it? What would you think of God's plan, then? What man would not descend into madness?"

I stared at the Archbishop.

His face flushed and he looked horrified.

"Please accept my apologies," he said. "That was utterly thoughtless of me."

"Of course," I said, wiping my eyes. I looked out at the sky. "How was it that Christians killed his wife? Why?"

He coughed and looked up at the ceiling for a moment. "Perhaps they were stopping to steal horses or simply looking for coin to pay for passage home before Saladin came. When it feels as though the rule of law is ending, men can forget God and instead look to earthly things for their salvation. They gather to them jewels and trinkets. The base instinct overwhelms their fear of God, their reason and their trust in the law. Or perhaps there was another reason. William seemed certain there was. Only God knows."

"Who were they?"

"The leader was noble. The others were common soldiers and when William had recovered from the first shock of his grief he hunted them down. As I recall, the leader ran to hide in Aragon. William stayed to hunt down all the others one by one. His madness was growing and he gathered those other monsters to him. I am ashamed to say that I thanked God when they left Outremer, even though I knew they were just taking their evil elsewhere. I have few contacts back in France any longer so that was the last I heard of him until William returned and started this bloody madness again."

A coldness had tight hold of my heart but I forced myself to ask the question. "The name. The name of the leader of the men who murdered William's wife."

"Yes," the Archbishop said, grim and nodding. "I see that you now know."

"The name," I said through gritted teeth, my hands gripping the arms of the chair.

"The man who killed William's family was Henry of Ashbury."

∞

On the second day from Acre we crossed into a great valley with high, rolling hills studded with dark green bushes and Antonius told us happily that we were on Saracen land. Most knights would have found such news to be disconcerting but we rode to find and kill William and his remaining men so the presence of a few thousand Saracens within a day's ride was of little concern.

"William drinks their blood, they say. He drinks it up and cuts their limbs from their bodies to better collect every drop." In the full light of the burning sun, Antonius the little Egyptian priest was as shrivelled as a date. Riding beside me on the road, he looked at me and grinned as he spoke, revelling in the horror of our expressions.

"Stop speaking," Adelard said, riding behind us with Elias, who was the other of the Archbishop's men.

We rode through a land as hot and dry as an oven. The road from Acre to Damascus had until recently been well travelled and yet we were the only people anywhere within sight or sound. It was hot and there had been drought for months so we went easy on our horses. Even though we feared ambush, my two men and I rode without wearing our hauberks or helmets because of the heat. My shield was slung across my back and at least it shaded me a little.

The road wound down along the side of the valley, crossed the dry river and wound back and forth through the distant hills to disappear over the horizon. Antonius, the priest, claimed William was hiding out beyond those hills so my intention had been to make camp there. We rested in the shade of a cliff through the middle of the day and we would push deep into them during the night. The moon would be almost full so travelling should be easier and it would be cool enough to comfortably wear our armour.

I hoped to catch William unawares in the darkness.

"William is no man," Antonius said. "He may have been a man once but he has been transformed. I think he is some other kind of being, perhaps."

"You think he is a demon?" I asked. "Surely you do not think he is Satan."

Antonius scratched his face and sighed. "No. I certainly do not say that William is Satan. But Satan was once an angel, hurled down from Heaven. The fallen angel is said to have taken other angels with him and these are the demons. Some are bound in darkness in everlasting chains but others walk the earth doing Satan's bidding. They delight in torment and pain and seek to undo God's will on earth."

"My lord," Adelard said. "Do we have to listen to this nonsense?"

Antonius grinned at me and turned back to smile at Adelard, which was inviting a severe beating.

"My whole life I have paid little attention to the priests," I said to Adelard. "But recently I have become interested in some of the stories."

Adelard said nothing and I glanced back in time to catch him rolling his eyes at Elias.

"Tell me about the Destroyer," I said to Antonius who looked startled. "William's men have referred to their master as such. But I do not understand."

Antonius shifted in his saddle and hesitated. "The Destroyer is called Exterminans. In Greek he is Abaddon. The angel of the abyss."

"Another demon?"

"No," Antonius cried. "No. He is the Angel that does the Lord's divine will. The Destroyer was sent by God to bring the plagues to Egypt. Some say the Destroyer is God's most loyal, most powerful aspect. They say that the Christ was the Destroyer sent to earth to bring destruction to the heathens, to the unjust and the unworthy."

Adelard grunted. "I never heard nothing like it before."

I had to agree with him.

"We follow the true way," Antonius snapped. "In Egypt."

Adelard looked offended and contemptuous. Elias looked disturbed.

"Be quiet now, priest," I said to him. "I have heard more than enough of your nonsense."

I glanced back and my men were smiling again. It was important I keep them happy for they were the only help I would have out there in the hills.

I had intended to hire as many men as I could. But the Archbishop and King Henry put a stop to that.

The two men I did have were burly enough. Adelard was older, Elias was his wife's nephew. Both were experienced and though Adelard was painfully slow his timing was faultless. Elias was fast as a snake but forever forgetting to raise his shield and both I and Adelard easily rapped him upon the head when we had fought mock duels while our preparations were made.

Neither man was happy. They had survived the crusade and until I had come along both had faced a future of easy work. I wondered if they would stand with me.

I was lost inside my grief and thoughts of my brother Henry. Charming Henry, the apple of our father's eye, who had travelled to the Holy Land on a pilgrimage and there committed the murder of a woman and a child. At first I could hardly credit what the Archbishop had revealed but the more I considered it, the less it surprised me.

Memories of Henry bubbled to the surface. Powerful, hateful Henry punching me to the ground as children, standing over me and cursing me until he was red in the face. I could not remember his words but I could quite clearly recall the look of mad savagery in his eyes. What had I done, I wondered, to deserve such spite?

There had always been some sort of feud between Henry and William. Henry was destined to swear fealty to William, just as our fathers had sworn to the de Ferrers back to the Conquest when my grandfather's grandfather was raised up and granted the Saxon hall at Ashbury. Perhaps it had started because they were close in age and both were proud and prickly boys.

Both had gone to the Holy Land but that was not unusual, even outside of a crusade. I always knew something had happened between my father and my brother for Henry to have suddenly run off. Whatever it was, Henry had murdered Earl William's family halfway across the world.

Perhaps it had been mere chance. Henry was fleeing the Saracen army, looking for loot and it happened to be William's undefended home. Desperate men can do evil things.

Still, there seemed to be a secret just out of reach. A secret that I could solve if I remembered hard enough, thought clearly enough.

Something in the present had been nagging at my thoughts as we crossed the dry river bed by way of the ancient stone bridge. Only after we had begun climbing out of the valley to the east was it that I noticed how Antonius kept glancing off up the hill. There was nothing there but jumbles of rocks and spiky bushes, with the clear sky above.

"Something catching your eye, Antonius?" I asked him.

"Oh, no, my lord," he said, smoothly. "Merely enjoying my freedom once again. Being a guest of your Archbishop for such long time has made me appreciate God's creation even more."

"Adelard," I said to him over my shoulder as we rode slowly, our horses" heads lowered. "Do you think we are being watched?"

Adelard snorted. "What, you just realised, lord?" he said.

"What makes you so sure?" I asked. His scorn, absurdly, had wounded me.

Elias swivelled his head, wide-eyed at the hills about us.

"The people are gone," Adelard said. "Empty homes mile after mile. If they'd ran off when they saw us coming we'd see cooking fires smoking and smell food. There's no livestock, either. We'd hear the goats if there were any for miles. And we have seen no travellers upon this road for many a mile."

"I believe you," I said. "But why does that mean we are being watched?"

"Lord, if the locals are gone then who is kicking up the dust in front and to the south?"

I peered at the sky in those directions. Perhaps there was a touch more dust there than elsewhere but I would have to trust on Adelard's experience.

"You know these lands, Antonius," I said, watching him closely. "Are we in any danger?"

He rubbed a skeletal finger along his nose. "Perhaps we are," he said, as if he had no cares either way. "Perhaps William's men are waiting for us. The road is notorious for surprise attacks." He coughed. "Perhaps we could ride down into the valley and along the valley floor. There is a way out up there across the pass at the end."

I nodded and looked up the length of the winding valley.

Far away at the head of the valley it rose up into an outcrop like the prow of a great ship, a flat deck at the top covered in rocks and scrub. Behind the flat area, the hill rose to a peak behind. It looked like a long, heavy climb.

"Perhaps," I said but the world had shifted again and I knew that the priest would have to be dealt with.

I kept us moving slowly with the rocky hills stretching above us on the right as it cut back and forth up the valley side. After a short while we rounded a cluster of huge boulders on the side of the road. My heart was racing at the thought of ambush waiting there but I had to deal with the priest. I pulled my horse up in the shade, shielded from view from anyone above. Antonius stopped further ahead and looked back.

"My horse is favouring a leg," I said, dismounting." I pulled my dagger and bent over, pulling a random hoof up. "A spine of some plant. In deep." I looked up at Adelard. "May as well dismount and rest, lads. Have a swig of Adam's Ale. I shall have to draw this slowly or I shall lame her."

Adelard and Elias were happy enough to stop but Antonius looked miserable. When a hot and thirsty man begrudges a few moments shade and a drink of water then something is very wrong indeed.

"Come soothe her while I draw it," I commanded the priest. He knew something was wrong but he came anyway.

I grabbed his scrawny shoulder, threw him against the wall of the boulder and put my dagger to his throat.

"What is waiting for us out there?" I said to him.

"How dare you?" Antonius said, as if he were baffled. "Take your filthy Frankish hands from me."

Adelard and Elias jumped to their feet. "Hold on to the horses," I told them. "Stay out of sight but watch both approaches."

They drew their swords and stood ready without a word.

I turned back to Antonius. "I will not ask again."

"The sun has baked your humours dry, lord," Antonius said, trying to grin. "Richard. My lord. I am a good Christian. I am helping you, yes?"

Perhaps my humours were dry but I knew he was lying. Was he in the pay of Saladin? Luring us into a trap to spark a war?

Whatever the truth, if I was ambushed and killed then William would go free and Alice, Isabella and their children and all the other innocents' deaths would go unpunished. Surely God would forgive anything I did in pursuit of my aim. He forgave Christians who killed Saracens for Christ so I was certain he would forgive me.

I slashed my dagger through his filthy, long robes. He flinched and chewed on his dry lips but held remarkably still while I cut and ripped a ragged strip of cloth from his sleeve and stuffed the lot into his mouth. He gagged repeatedly until I slapped him, hard.

His eyes were white all the way round and they swam out of focus from the blow to his head so I waited until they fixed upon me once more.

"I am afraid that I must cut into your flesh now, Antonius. I shall do this in the hope that you understand how much the success of this quest means to me," I explained. "And after I have cut into your flesh I shall remove this cloth from your mouth and then you shall explain to me what is waiting for us up in the hills here."

He began moaning, speaking with rapid hums from his throat.

"It's no good trying to talk now," I said, shaking my head as if I was heartbroken. "You had your chance. You can tell me all about it when I am done. I promise you that I take no joy in this and I regret its necessity immensely."

Taking my dagger, I sliced a deep cut along the outside of his forearm. He whimpered and shuddered as the sun-baked skin split aside to let the gloriously red blood well up and pour out along it. His eyes were wide as he stared at it dripping into the pale dust.

Next I cut into his left shoulder. There was no fat there. I cut through just skin and bone in a line from his collarbone right around to his shoulder blade. Blood gushed out. Antonius's breath was whistling in and out of his nostrils.

The third cut I sliced deep into the skin on his face under his left eye, opening it down to the cheekbone. He whimpered and shuddered as the blood welled and ran down in a steady stream.

I pulled the cloth from his mouth and he vomited thick bile and then gagged repeatedly until I shoved him upright, cracking his head against the rock.

"Now you get to tell me the truth," I said, smiling.

The hatred that filled his eyes was startling. "You are doing the bidding of the Angel of the Lord. He has called and you have come. And he will drink the blood of your—"

"Not this again." I kicked him in the balls and he fell to the ground, winded and writhing. That, at least, shut him up.

"Let us put on our mail," I said to my men who were both staring at me with a look somewhere between horror and newfound respect. "The priest is William's man after all and we should expect his bastards to attack us on the road."

We helped each other into our doublets and hauberks.

"We are a mere two days from Acre, lord," Adelard said once we stood ready. His tone was humbler than it had been before. "A day if we ride through the night."

"You may go where you think is best," I said to them. "But I swore an oath and there can be no turning back for me."

They stared.

"We are here because of a ruse, lord," Adelard said slowly. "Surely you know it would be madness to continue?"

"We know they are waiting for us," Elias explained, as if I was simple-minded.

I nodded. "And I shall fight my way through and on to William's hiding place. There, with God's will, I shall cut off his head with this sword."

A deranged chuckling coughed its way out from the curled-up priest. "He cannot be killed. He will never die. For he is God's final prophet and God shall bring about the—"

I kicked him in the stomach so hard he stopped breathing. After a long moment, he juddered into movement again, wheezing like a broken bellows.

My men whispered and gestured to each other while I waited.

Whether it was honour, a sense of duty to the Archbishop, the Kingdom of Jerusalem or that they believed their chances were better beside me than riding back by themselves, they elected to head on with me and Antonius.

The priest I gagged, lest he cry out and give us away and

I tied it in place around his head. I tied the rest of him up tight, too, with wrists tied together and then tied hard against his belly. Then I sat him back on his horse and left a few yards of rope to hold on to, lest he attempt to ride away.

I left his wounds open and bleeding. I had no doubt his cuts would become infected but then as soon as I found William I was going to kill the priest anyway. His poor horse was disturbed by the blood but she calmed after some reassurance.

"How many?" I asked him again before we moved off. "Nod your head once for each man waiting to ambush us."

He shook his head.

"If you do not tell me how many of them there are then when the fighting begins yours shall be the first throat that gets cut," I ventured.

He shook his head again, mad eyes shining.

My men shrugged and I had to agree with them. When slicing a man open does not cause him to talk then there is not much more one can do without a range of sharp implements, a lot of time and a special kind of creativity.

"Let us try a different route," I said. "Along the floor of the valley by the river." I pointed.

"That is the way he wanted us to go," Adelard said.

"Quite right," I said, looking at the huge promontory

high up at the head of the valley.

I wanted to ride into William's trap. I longed for his men to attack us. I wanted to kill those men and I wanted them to lead me to William.

As long as I found success, I did not care if I lived to see the coming dawn.

But I did not say such things to my own two men. Having no true idea of what I rode toward, I thanked God for their company.

"Come on," I said.

We rode down into the valley.

CHAPTER EIGHT
VALLEY OF
DEATH

WE AMBLED ALONG THE VALLEY as the sun fell lower and lower toward the hills to the west.

I expected to get an arrow through the neck at any moment. I imaged what it would be like to look down and see an arrowhead poking through my chest, glinting with shiny blood.

Below us the riverbed was dry but for patches of mud and isolated pools with areas of tall plants growing. Despite the drought, the land all around us was green and good for some crops and goats. Adelard said the water for the valley came from springs. Far behind us out of sight beyond the hills to the South was the Sea of Galilee. It was likewise forever filled by the springs even when the river ran dry and the rains did not fall. And there were trees. Spindly things with pale bark and small dark leaves but there were plenty of copses all over the valley. Copses dense enough to hide a group of horsemen.

It was ancient land. Here and there stood stubs of walls or stones with remnants of ancient carving upon their faces. Long ago there had been wealth in the hills. Now it was a land of scattered houses, sometimes gathered in clusters. It had been much ravaged by war. The sight of Frankish knights would have been enough to cause them to flee but it seemed that everyone had been gone for quite some time.

Damascus was merely sixty or seventy miles to the north-east. Although we were off the main road there should have been people moving around within and along the valley. There was no-one.

The heat of the day finally faded. The road climbed up the eastern side, away from the relative lushness below. We came closer to that high rocky promontory that jutted out above the riverbed and hills below. A single man up there could keep watch over miles of country. Our road lead there.

The surface of the road showed heavy use. Dusty hoof and cart tracks had kicked and rolled through the dried, cracked earth.

"What's this?" I asked.

The dust had been greatly disturbed and there was a scatter of bark and tiny twigs.

Adelard peered at it. "Nothing, lord. A load of logs fell off a wagon, that's all."

It was quiet even in the scattered villages on the other side of the valley. The sun fell behind the hills to our left. The sky was yet bright but we rode through shadow. Other than the warm wind it was deathly quiet and I saw no movement and heard no sound of pursuit.

I prayed that William was close.

We came to a spring that bubbled from a stone-lined crevice. Water ran trickling down the hill in a narrow ditch toward the huge riverbed below us. A little brown bird like a sparrow fluttered about in it, ducking its head under and shaking itself.

"We should make camp here," Adelard said and Elias nodded. Their heads swivelled back and forth up and down the hill and both repeatedly looked behind us.

"Water the horses. We camp there," I said, pointing to the high outcrop looming above us.

They were deeply unhappy at the prospect of the climb.

I hoped that they would not be too tired to fight when we reached the top.

Antonius was drifting in and out of wakefulness. The blood from his wounds had mostly dried hard. Sometimes he was jostled by his horse over uneven ground and he would jerk his wounds open and they wept afresh. The flies could not believe their luck and swarmed him. I wondered if he would live to reach the top.

Night proper fell. The sky fading into black.

It was a long climb in the dark and we had little strength left for discussion. We trusted the horses to feel their way up. It was unkind and foolhardy to push them further but I wanted time to set up a proper defence. My men also needed rest. Adelard was puffing and blowing as much as his mare.

The moon rose and cast a beautiful silver light brighter than a midwinter noon back in Ashbury.

Our horses were breathing hard when we wound our way out to a flat shelf near to the top of the hill. Crisscrossing stone walls had been left to crumble into ruin. To the rear of the shelf of land the hill rose abruptly to a scrubby peak fifty or a hundred feet further up. There was a foul smell in the air, like a goat had fallen into a cave and rotted.

I assumed the ruins had once been a watch tower with a

few outer walls. It was a perfect place for one. Even in moonlight the view was magnificent.

My men were ready to drop but without rest or complaint began unburdening the horses. The poor creatures were all shaking so Elias said he would walk them about before allowing them to drink.

"Keep watch," I commanded Adelard and he went to lean on one of the ruined walls, peering out at the valley. His battered old shield slung across his back.

I dragged Antonius the deceiver from his horse with the rope around his waist and he fell, hard. He whimpered. I tied the trailing end of it tight around his ankles. Then yanked them tight so that his ankles were bent up to his backside. I bound them to his waist. He was a scrawny streak of piss but that did not mean he was not dangerous. I could not afford to take chances. When he was secure I pulled the strip of cloth from out of his mouth.

"Please," he said, his throat sounded dry as wind-blown sand. Even though it was night, black flies buzzed on his scabrous wounds.

I left him bound upon the dusty rock, pulled the cork from my precious skin of water and held it near to his face. Sticking out his tongue he gasped for a drop.

"When you tell me what I want to know," I said. "I will allow you to drink this whole skin of water."

His eyes told me he did not believe me which was fair of him because I was lying.

"He will come for all of you and he will eat your children," Antonius mumbled past cracked lips.

I sighed and looked out down the valley through which we had ascended. The moonlight edged every rock and bush in silver and cast moon shadow ribbons between the dotted lines of trees. It was bright enough to see fields and houses. Far off was a jagged black band under the silver black sky.

"Where are all the people?" I asked Antonius.

He smiled, cracking his lips and wincing as the blood seeped from the cracks. "Serving a higher cause," he said, throat rasping.

"Horsemen," Adelard said from the edge. "Riding slow, following our way."

Elias immediately ran by me to join Adelard.

"How many?" I asked.

"Five," Adelard said.

"Seven?" Elias said.

"What in God's name's wrong with you, boy?" Adelard said and clouted the back of his head before turning round to me. "Perhaps as few as four, lord."

"Not much of an ambush, is it," I said.

"Our horses will never survive a pursuit, lord," Elias said.

"Four is nothing," I boasted. "This is a good place. We

shall stand here. How long do we have?"

"They're a fair way off yet," Adelard said.

"We could keep on by walking our horses out of the valley northwards," Elias said, pointing. "Theirs will be blown by the climb, too, we can stay ahead of them."

I crouched down with Antonius. He eyed the dagger at my waist and licked his lips, tongue rasping over the sores. Clearly the trap was being sprung so I held the mouth of the skin to his mouth and squirted in the tepid spring water. He sucked it down like a babe on the breast until I took it away. I wanted him able to speak but not sated. The bastard could suffer. And I needed every advantage, no matter how small.

"William sent you to Acre to lead men to him?" I said.

Antonius savoured the water for a moment, sighing. "He sent me to the Archbishop, yes. My lord wished me to get soldiers," he shrugged. "Or priests."

"But why? We could have brought a hundred men down upon him, had the Archbishop chosen to do so. Why would William risk his destruction by sending you?"

The men were listening but kept keeping watch over the edge.

"He swore to us that they would not send many," Antonius said, eyes shining. "And he spoke the truth, did he not? My lord sees things mortal men cannot see. He is the light of the world and his blood is the light of the life."

"Yes, yes," I said. "But why lure anyone at all?"

"My lord seeks new brothers to join us," Antonius said. "Our numbers must grow, my lord says, if we are to bring his revelations to all the people of God's land. You shall see, all of you shall see and then you shall follow him as faithfully as I have and you will be rewarded with everlasting life on earth."

Adelard laughed from over by the edge. "Why in God's name would we join with William?"

"Once you received his Eucharist," Antonius said, mad eyes shining in the moonlight. "Then you will know the truth. I was like you. I doubted. I was on my knees looking up with contempt and pity for his evil. But once I tasted it, I became filled with the strength and the power of God made flesh."

"His Eucharist?" I asked.

"His holy blood is fire in your veins," Antonius said, his voice rising in passion. "I was old and weak and then I was strong." The priest coughed and winced and his voice fell to a whisper. "But the Gift fades, day by day. Every Sabbath we share the sacrament. It has been so very long since I drank from him. I am so hungry. So very hungry."

Adelard and Elias looked as confused and disturbed as I felt.

The wind was full of dust and the smell of juniper. Our horses whinnied and stamped their feet, nervous. They snorted. Perhaps it was the smell of the priest; that old and new blood and the beginnings of rotting flesh.

There was a sound. Faint enough to almost be the wind but not quite. It reminded me of a millstone in use. I stood and looked across the intersecting ruin of walls for the source but saw nothing in the deep shadows. After just a moment the sound was no more.

"Adelard, Elias. Listen to me," I said, speaking softly and they turned around. "This was always the place of ambush. Those men in the valley are but one part of it. Others will be coming from the north. Elias, get my shield and your own."

But both men jumped in surprise and drew their swords, staring behind me. At the same time I heard footsteps approaching and I leapt to my feet and spun round, drawing my own blade.

Five men approached in the darkness spread in a wide row, stepping carefully across the ruins. They took up position, arrayed before us.

In the centre was Hugo the Giant.

He stood flanked by two Saracen knights. They held their curved swords already drawn and at the ready. To either side of those Saracens were two crossbowmen of the

Italian style, with their weapons loaded and aimed us.

All the men were filthy. The stench of stale blood and rotten meat was so bad I could not believe I had failed to smell them on the wind as they had approached.

A slow chuckle emerged from Hugo's belly, deep as a rumble of thunder.

"It is too late to flee, Richard of Ashbury," the voice said. "You belong to the Destroyer now. Come with me."

"Hugo the Giant," I said, my heart hammering in my chest at the thought of fighting such a monster. "I have come to bring justice to Earl William de Ferrers. I shall slay you also. As I will Hugh of Havering, Roger of Tyre and any man that stands against me."

He stood grim faced and unmoved by my words. The Saracens and crossbowmen also stood and stared. The crossbows did not waver. One pointed at me, the other at Adelard or Elias over my shoulder.

I knew crossbows. A man can learn to shoot one in very little time. They are simple to point and squeeze and at close range a bolt will punch through mail and bury deep into flesh. Even a boy could use one with ease and the men with Hugo were experienced specialists.

Hugo the Giant spoke French with a strange accent and I recalled that he was from Antioch. "Come," he said, his voice a landslide. "I swear you will be safe if you come with me. My lord loves you and wishes that you join with him. If you do not you shall be sacrificed to him and your blood will feed him and he will feed us with his Blessed Sacrament."

One weakness of the crossbow was that you could pull too hard to release the bolt and then miss the target. This tended to happen when a man was panicking. The other weakness was the length of time they took to reload.

"He loves us?" I asked, picking a single drop from the torrent of madness simply to keep Hugo talking while my men shuffled behind me. I prayed that they would fight.

Hugo shook his giant head. "The Angel of the Lord has sent for you and you have come to him as—"

I threw myself forward at the crossbowman on the farthest left. By moving outward I hoped to stay away from Hugo long enough to kill his men. I looped around then changed direction and charged right at the man pointing a sharp steel headed bolt at me.

I roared a wordless battle cry and wheeled my sword over my head like a maniac. He panicked and squeezed the mechanism too early. I danced further left as he pulled. The weapon clacked and the bolt ripped through the air by my head. The crossbowman hesitated, reached for another bolt, thought better of it and raised his crossbow ready to block my attack. But anything other than immediate flight had been his final mistake. For I ran by him and swung the edge of my blade into his throat, crushing it into pulp. He fell, dying.

The other crossbow clanked too but the bolt shot toward Adelard or Elias. Both charged the other side of the enemy line.

I kept moving. The nearest Saracen knight closed in on me with Hugo looming behind him, striding around to the other side of me. I had to kill the knight before facing Hugo. Or I knew I was dead.

Heart slamming in my chest I closed on the Saracen, thrusting with the point of my sword to push him back away from Hugo. I had to isolate him, drive him from the others. Hugo was behind me and my fear of that giant threatened to overwhelm me. Still I pushed the attack. The Saracen gave ground.

Hugo the Giant charged in like a bullock. The giant's arms were long, his sword was longer than mine own and it was twice as wide. So I had to duck and dance away from his powerful swings without ever being close enough to harm him. And so the Saracen closed on me again. Changing my direction I swung my blade toward Hugo. He checked his attack and blocked my sword with the edge of his. It was like hitting a boulder. The shock of it rang through my bones into my skull. I was afraid my blade would break and shatter but it remained whole. I retreated backward, my teeth aching from the impact. Hugo's face was expressionless as he stalked after me, poking his blade at my face. I fended him off. The Saracen came at me full charge and I deflected and countered with a flurry of blows. He blocked or dodged them, blades clashing in the night. My sword was being dented and blunted and I cursed myself for not having a shield.

The Saracen was so fast. The unnatural speed of his sword arm and footwork was just as it had been when William's men killed me in my hall. As full of fire as he was, there was not much skill in the man and I would have bested him but for Hugo. The giant pushed forward and kept me from getting away. He was so slow but skilful and possessed an inhuman strength. So I kept my distance. I was faster than he was, faster even than the Saracen and I kept them both away. My point jabbed into the Saracen's shoulder, hard, and he reeled away with a shout. The Saracen looked to Hugo, confused and clutching the point I had struck.

Hugo stopped. He looked at his Saracen. He looked at me. He had the tiniest fraction of expression on his face, something like curiosity or confusion. "You move like he does," Hugo said, his voice like an iron door slamming in Hell. "How is that possible?"

I stamped my foot forward to feign an attack and drive him away so I could finish the Saracen. But just then one of my men cried out. I glanced toward Adelard and Elias. I did it so briefly that I could see nothing other than figures fighting across the far side of the rock platform. We were too far to help or hinder each other.

A glance was all it took. I was distracted enough for Hugo to decide to come at me, bellowing like thunder. It was immediately clear that Hugo's relative slowness had been a trick. He was actually just as fast as his Saracen was. In fright I swiped his huge sword away, the impact jarring me to the teeth again. I stepped back into the path of the Saracen's blade. That sneaking Saracen swept a glancing blow into my back, slicing his curved edge down the mail.

Such a blow could not cut me for my mail protected against cuts. But the force of the impact was enough to snap ribs and knock the breath from my body. And it threw me off balance. I ducked and swayed away from their blades in something close to panic, certain that I was going to die and stepped backwards as fast as I could, my heartbeat hammering in my ears and my breathing rattling my ribs.

I never saw the wall behind me. A little stub as high as my calves that sent me flying backwards. The hard earth slammed into my broken ribs and cracking into the back of my helm.

The Saracen leapt the wall and his blade sang toward my face. I swung my sword wildly, knocking his aside and kicked out at his knee as he landed on that leg. There was a loud pop as the bones there snapped and his knee crunched as the shards ground against each other. He fell on top of me, his helmeted head crashing into mine. My sword was gone and he was so close I could feel his hot breath on my face. Grabbing his head with both hands to hold him to me I sunk my teeth into his cheek and bit down as hard as I could. I was astonished that my teeth bit through his beard and muscle right through to his cheekbone. He screamed in my ear and jerked up away from me, pulling a strip of flesh off his cheek and spilling hot blood into my mouth. I held his head, biting down harder and he thrashed his head about trying to get away which simply served to tear his cheek right off his face. I had a glimpse of shining, bloody teeth and skull inside and I had to swallow the blood and drool that gushed into my mouth, lest I drown in it.

Hugo yanked the screaming Saracen away as if he were a child, tossed him down beside me still screaming and thrust down at my chest with his sword. I twisted my body sideways, rolling from the blow so that it sprang against the stones that had been under me. Immediately I rolled back onto the blade, trapping it against my mailed back and kept rolling until I was flat on my back. The blade bent but it could only flex so far and the sword was levered from Hugo's grasp and flung out to the side.

I reached for my own blade laying just out of reach but Hugo yanked a dagger from his belt and sank toward me. He was monstrously heavy but he had about seven feet to descend and I was fast and filled with fury so I grasped his wrist, which was as wide as a ham and held the blade away from me. The rest of his body smashed into me and I felt more ribs popping in my chest as his knee landed, the breath squeezed out of me and I thought my heart would burst.

But I held on. More than held on, I forced his wrist and the blade it held away from me to the side. Hugo finally allowed his face to show something; astonishment.

I used his own momentum to throw him over with my hips and rolled him over and down onto the Saracen who was shrieking and cupping the hole where that half of his face had been. I twisted the dagger from Hugo's massive hands and smashed his face with my armoured forehead. Again and again I struck him until he stopped moving and then I stopped. His head was like a horse's; the bone of his skull as thick as stone and I wondered if I had smashed my own brains out.

Underneath his body the Saracen squirmed, trying to get out so I snatched up Hugo's dagger and stabbed it into the

Saracen's throat to silence him.

Hugo's face and skull was partly caved in but he was not dead. His massive hands groped blindly up towards my head. I stabbed the blade through the smashed cracks around Hugo's eyes and into his brain over and over again. His hands fell away.

Only when I ran out of breath was it I realised I had been screaming.

I rolled from Hugo and fell down next to the bodies, my chest heaving, not sure what damage I had received. The Saracen knight and Hugo lay next to me one atop the other.

There were two others I had not killed. Another Saracen and a crossbowman had been fighting my men. Cursing and wincing I looked for my sword.

Footsteps scraped toward me in the dark from the other side of the low wall that I had fallen over and I scrambled to my sword and swung it up toward Adelard's face. He blocked it with his shield. There was a crossbow bolt sticking into it. I let out the breath I was holding.

"You are alive," I said, stupidly.

There was blood all over his head and hands. But it was not his.

"Elias is dead," he said.

Together they had killed the other Saracen knight and the crossbowman but not before Elias had been pierced through the chest with the bolt. He had drowned and suffocated after killing the man who had shot him.

"Fast pair of bastards, they were," Adelard said, shaking his head.

Antonius still lay tied up on his side, head craned up looking at me with fear in his eyes. That, at least, made me feel happy.

"There's still those other men on horseback heading up here for us," Adelard said. There was a black rage in him and he wanted more men to kill.

I was hurt from the fight and limped over to him. The monstrous weight of Hugo falling upon me had crushed my ribs and my back ached and I knew I would be massively bruised. But the thought of another fight to come made the pain melt away. My mouth still tasted of the Saracen's blood. I felt it all roiling in my otherwise-empty belly and somehow I began to feel better. Strength returned to my limbs and my breathing slowed.

"How skilled are you with a crossbow?" I asked Adelard as he stood looking down at the bloody corpse that was once Elias.

"Held one a few years ago," Adelard said. He was breathing hard. There's nothing in all the world so tiring as battle and it was remarkable I was not more exhausted.

"Then I shall take both weapons," I said and we gathered

them, along with a half-dozen bolts and I stood at the point where the road reached the top of the plateau. The point where our pursuers would emerge. "You take your shield and wait behind that corner of wall. Ensure that they see you after they reach the top."

I gagged Antonius again, dragged him squirming into deep shadow. I hid behind the walls beside the top of the path and glanced over the edge. The horsemen were climbing slowly but the scraping of their horse's hoofs and clashing of their armour grew ever closer.

We did not have long to wait.

I was certain that they would have heard the fighting from atop our rock outcrop, the sounds travelling easily in the still night air. They would have heard it and then heard the silence that followed.

There were merely four of them after all. So certain their friends would have defeated us that they called out for them in the foreign tongue of the Saracens. No doubt they were imagining rest and sustenance awaiting them at the top and that was good for if men are unprepared for a fight then they make easy prey. They trudged up, making a huge noise and at the top of the hill they tied up their blowing horses near to our own.

I was in shadow but they came so close that if anyone turned in my direction they would see the gleam of the bolt upon my loaded bow, as well as the other loaded one sat ready upon the wall before me. I could smell the sweat and the stench of horse from the men in the warm night wind but I held my shot until they had stumbled closer into our trap.

They called out, becoming nervous that their friends were not responding to their hails.

One of them saw Adelard duck his head down behind the ruined wall and cried out a warning. I jumped up and shot a bolt into his lower back. He grunted and went down with his sword half out of his scabbard.

The other three were frozen in indecision when Adelard ran around the wall then charged toward them with his shield up and growling some guttural war cry. I shot another of them in the centre of the spine and he fell straight down like when you drop a rope. I tossed that second bow away and leapt over the wall.

A small part of me felt sympathy for the way the two remaining men turned to run from Adelard just to come face to face with me bearing down on them.

It was small part of me only. The rest of me was filled with a cool rage and I cut one down without hesitation. He hardly had time to scream when I smashed his head in with my sword. The idiot was not wearing a helmet.

I allowed Adelard to cut the other man down. The

Saracen was staring up at me in confusion and terror when Adelard smashed him in the side of the head. I stood and watched as Adelard stabbed all four men in the throat with the point of his sword, just to be sure.

"Got to bury Elias now, lord," Adelard said. "Can't leave him for the vultures."

"Fine," I said, stretching my back. The Christian thing to do was bury him, I supposed but I was not going to waste my strength on it. "Pile up stones to cover him. You will never get through this ground." Adelard should not have wasted his strength either and if I'd been a harder man, as hard a man as I later became, then I would have forced him to abandon his friend's internment.

As it was, while he grunted and clanked rocks about I searched the ruins for the place where Hugo and his Saracens had crept out from. I had been distracted talking to Antonius when they appeared but there was no chance those five men had snuck up from any great distance and I knew there must be a way into the hill under our feet. There were too many shadows for me to find it without knowing where to look.

"Dear God," Adelard said, standing at the head of the cairn he had built against one wall over the young man's body. I went to join him. "Elias was just a lad. He never wanted much from life. To tell the truth he was half simple.

But he was a good fighter. He never did nothing bad. He's the sort of man you want up there, Lord. Amen."

"Amen," I said and tried to remember that this man's death was on William's hands, not my own.

"Don't know how I'm going to tell my wife about this," Adelard said in a whisper. "Promised I'd take care of him."

"Go drink and eat, if you can," I said.

"Good advice," Adelard said. "You should take it yourself, lord."

The blood in my belly seemed sustenance enough so I patted him on his shoulder and then stood over Antonius. "I swore that I was going to kill you should we be ambushed."

He looked up, eyes shining.

"You will lead me to where William is. If you tell me the truth and help me then I swear I shall not harm you. If you lie or lead me astray I shall bury a blade in your heart. Do you understand?"

He nodded and I took the gag from his mouth.

"We should kill him now, lord," Adelard said, chewing bread. "He's no priest."

"But I am," Antonius said. "Saladin's men sent me to Acre to tell your people that the attacks on the caravans and pilgrims were not of his doing. I spoke French, I was a Christian, and they said I would be trusted. But I was taken on the road, brought before William. And then I saw."

I shrugged. "William has Saracens fighting for him?"

"Saracens," Antonius scoffed. "An idiotic word. Our lord's followers were once Franks, Kurds, Turks, Arabs, Egyptians. Any man who drinks from him, no matter what he was before, sees the truth once they taste his blood."

"How many followers?" I asked. "How many are knights?"

Antonius screwed his face up. "Twenty? Thirty? I never counted."

Adelard groaned. "Lord, we must return with more men."

I ignored him.

"You said before that you take William's Eucharist," I said, prompting Antonius.

"He saw in me that I was ready to receive the sacraments. The blood of Christ straight from William's veins. It filled my arms with such power, such strength. My mind was sharpened like a sabre. My body was fast as a striking snake and strong as a lion. My wounds were healed in an instant. My eyes saw through this world to the edge of the next one. And I knew. I understood. Before me stood the cup of Christ in the form of a man."

"You all drink the blood from William's veins on the Sabbath?" I said. "Thirty of you?"

Antonius sneered. "Of course it is on the Sabbath. Unless the men are sent out to raid," he said, bitterly. "Then they get it before they depart."

"What day is it today?" I asked Adelard.

"Saturday, lord," he said then looked at the sky. "Sunday, now, I suppose."

I looked through the darkness to where the bodies of Hugo and the other men lay waiting for the sun to bring thousands of flies to feast and lay eggs in their flesh.

"Drinking his blood makes a man faster?" I asked Antonius. "Stronger?"

Antonius grinned. "Strong with the power of God."

"And William's knights also drink the blood of the innocent? Why?"

He shrugged. "It prolongs and increases the effects of the sacrament."

"Can it really be?" I asked, almost to myself.

"You shall see," Antonius said, giggling. "Oh yes, you shall see when you drink from him that the Christ has come again in the form of William, the Angel of the Lord, the Destroyer."

Adelard cleared his throat. "Should he not be slain for such blasphemy?" He could barely contain himself. "Calling this evil the Eucharist, lord? It offends God."

"You swore you would not harm me if I spoke truth,"

Antonius said, squirming away, full of fear.

"He should be slain," I said to Adelard. "But not by us. I swore an oath."

Adelard spat to show what he thought of that. And he was quite right but still I cut the ropes about Antonius" waist and ankles and, with Adelard's sword at his back, he led us to a square cut into the bedrock in the corner of some ruined walls. It was the same size and shape as a grave. There was a slab beside it that Hugo must have pushed out of the way before climbing up to ambush us.

The black rectangle had rock-cut steps at the nearest edge leading down into darkness.

"It stinks," Adelard said.

The air coming up from the hole reeked of death. I recognised the smell in the air, now, the smell I had detected as I had reached the head of the valley. It was the wet foulness of fresh blood, mixed with wood smoke. Fresh blood and the corruption of old death, too.

"What is waiting for us down there?" I asked Antonius while Adelard lit a torch.

"Death."

Adelard stared at me, his eyes pits of inky blackness flickering with reflected yellow torch light. I felt as though I should tell him everything would be well and to trust in God but in truth I agreed with the priest. The stench of death was pouring out of from the entire hill. It stank of butchery and battlefields. My stomach churned again.

"There may be death down there," I said, drawing that withered old creature so close to me I could smell the dried blood and stale piss on him. "But I shall bring even more."

He grinned.

The three of us descended the steps into the depths of the mountain.

CHAPTER NINE

CAVERN OF

BLOOD

DARKNESS. OUR STEPS ECHOED on the stone underfoot through the long, narrow tunnel that led down into the hill.

Adelard's torch gave off a hot light behind. He held it up close to the natural stone ceiling but still I trod into blackness with my shield raised and the point of my sword before me.

The air was smoky. That foul wind blew through the passageway, guttering the torch and carrying with it that stench of dank corruption.

My eyes played tricks with the darkness. I could see swirling shapes ahead that vanished. There were distant voices like whispers on the wind. Antonius' breath was loud behind me. Adelard's laboured panting threatened to overwhelm any noise I might hear ahead. It was as though I could smell his fear and hear his heart clangouring against his ribs.

With every step, I feared falling into a spike pit or stumbling into an ambush from the walls either side. Surely, I reasoned, they would have heard the fighting atop their lair? Surely, they would send men looking for Hugo and the others?

But William was up ahead. He had to be. And nothing was going to stop me. I was so close and all the hesitant shuffling forward seemed absurd.

I stopped and sheathed my sword.

"What is it?" Adelard hissed.

"Antonius goes first," I whispered. "And if you know of anything waiting for us ahead, speak before we reach it or you shall die before I do."

"I told you," Antonius said, his voice echoing. "Only death waits for—"

I slapped the words from his mouth, span him round and pushed him before me down the tunnel. Adelard ran to catch up behind me. I hurried forward, pushing Antonius at close to a running pace, ready to drop to a knee and raise my shield at the first sign of danger.

It seemed that the tunnel went deeper, downhill, but I could not be certain. Every so often there was a whiff of cool night air from cracks in the rock or from other tunnels and shafts. We rounded bends and corners until I was utterly disoriented. I knew not what direction we walked. Nor how far we had gone. When we got further in I thought I saw doorways cut every so often passing beside me; black, cold yawning maws with no life down them.

Soon there were voices, growing louder. The smell of smoke and death was stronger and Antonius slowed.

Light ahead. Flickering lamp light on the wall of the tunnel.

I suppose I should have waited. I should have crept forward, taken my time to assess and devised a plan with Adelard. But I was certain William was close. And I was so filled with rage that I shoved Antonius onward toward it ever faster.

The tunnel ended in a sharp turn to the left and there was an arched entranceway hewn into the bedrock. Beyond was a huge cavern where the lamp light spilled from. I dragged Antonius to a halt and peeked a little way in.

The cavern was lined with ancient wooden beams and

planks around the edges, presumably for holding back rock falls. The ceiling above was lost in darkness. I stepped forward toward the opening and saw deeper inside. It was as long as the nave of Acre's cathedral church.

"Lord," Adelard said behind me, caution in his voice.

"Watch the priest," I said to him.

Hefting my shield and readying my sword, I strode into the huge space. And froze.

The stench hit me first. A thick, cloying taste of blood on the air; like a battlefield. Like Ashbury manor house, like my own hall, after William.

The far end of the cavern was lit up by a roaring fire in a brazier. The bonfire was at waist height, blazing upon a vast iron bowl, supported by three legs.

Men moved down there at the far end of the cavern before the fire. Many stripped to the waist or naked. Some carried fuel for the fire, others heaved bodies around a large stone cistern in the centre of the floor. More stood and watched. Chains hung down from the ceiling, clicking against each other. One of the chains ended in a terribly long hook of the sort used to hang meat or a cauldron over a fire. The floor shone with fresh blood.

The light threw everyone into half silhouette. The long space between me and them was in shadow.

A man stirred to one side down by my feet.

He had been laying by the door in the shadow. There was a lamp on an alcove above him and from the corner of my eye I saw him jump into wakefulness. As a cry of warning began in his chest I ran him through, pushing the point through his ribs and into his heart. He stared at me, astonished and offended and in utter disbelief. A poor excuse for a guard.

"Sweet suffering Christ," Adelard muttered at my shoulder, staring down the cavern.

I turned back. My feet rooted as one man dragged a struggling figure from somewhere behind the brazier. He dragged them toward the big cistern.

They came into the light from the fire. The man was Hugh of Havering. The struggling figure was a woman. She was naked, old, begging and sobbing.

Hugh fought her, struck her senseless, got his hands on her hips and heaved her up onto the hooked chain. She writhed and groaned and tried to pry his hands from her. The huge hook pierced her back. She screamed once but the weight of her body bore her down and punched the spike through to burst from her chest and she was silent.

Another man pulled the other end of the chain from by the wall and she lifted higher up, her feet raised above head height. Blood welled out of her, ran down her skin and gushed from her toes into the cistern below her, spattering all around it. The fountain of blood was lit from behind by the fire. The woman jerked around like a fish on a line and the man who had hung her upon it reached up and tugged her down, hard. The hook sunk deeper inside her chest cavity with an audible crunch and she stopped moving again. The blood kept coming.

"Bring another one." The familiar, dreaded voice echoed around the cavern. "One of the children, I think. I can wait no longer."

William.

I had heard him but could not see him down there. But knowing he was there was enough for the rage to fill me.

Before I had left Jaffa for Acre I had stopped at Alice's tomb. I had begged her forgiveness and promised her justice for her and for her sweet children. Another oath that was no more than meaningless words unless it was fulfilled. I remembered her eyes fixed upon mine as William had sunk his teeth into her neck.

It was only when I was halfway across the cavern that I realised I was charging the men.

I had my sword in hand, my shield up before me. My own breathing in my ears, my hauberk jangling and my footsteps slapping on the ground.

God be with me, I prayed.

There were warning cries as I burst into the fire light by

the cistern. A filthy man beside me leapt up in panic and tried to run away but I speared my sword through his neck and bore him down under me.

William's men, the murderers in that cavern of blood were not armoured and most held no weapon. And yet many of them came right at me, full of mad fury and seemed ready and willing to tear me apart with their bare hands.

My sword slashed left and right and I kept moving and slamming men with my shield and stabbing them. Few were killing strokes but their naked skin split to the bone from strokes that mail would have turned away. My sword was like lightning, leaping from the flesh of one man into another. One or two men ducked through a doorway but I knew not where they went.

They were not fast. They were not lightning quick as the men up top had been. And I was faster than I had ever been and filled with a mad fury of my own.

Men collapsed, screaming, all around me and survivors laying upon the blood-soaked floor would not be long for the world. I edged through them, moving deeper in, heading towards the fire.

When I reached the cistern I stopped. The woman's body swung back and forth above, blood still trickling down her skin from the hook wound to drip and run from her toes.

I saw William.

There, finally. Standing to one side and behind the raised brazier where he was hidden in its glare. He was smiling.

More of his men came toward me. These ones had grabbed their weapons from that that side room and were coming to kill me. A couple of them had banged a helmet onto their head but otherwise were also unarmoured. Swords, maces and spears swung and stabbed at me. Blows struck me in the shoulder and the leg and they were powerful but I kept moving around the cistern, back and forth. A man tried to trip me with his spear but I trod on it and stabbed through his loins in the same movement. A crossbow clanked and the bolt bounced from my shield to my helmet and then I killed the man who had shot from one knee.

I killed them all until just a handful remained. Those men did not rush in. There were six of them and they spread out slowly around me.

One was Hugh of Havering, William's right hand man. Another was Roger of Tyre. These were men I wanted to kill. But not as much as I wanted to eviscerate their lord.

"Fight me yourself," I shouted at William.

He smiled and shook his head, as if I had invited him to share a cup of ale at the village fair.

"Coward," I shouted.

William laughed. "I feared you would never come."

His men kept circling; two of them moving behind me. One of them, a great bearded lump of a Saracen hefted a huge two handed axe. Hugh and Roger stayed between me and William.

"Nothing could keep me from killing you," I said.

He tilted his head. "Not even your own death, Richard?"

He nodded to his men and they charged in all together.

There is no way to defend yourself against six skilled, armed men. It is impossible.

So I attacked.

I twisted from William, from Hugh and Roger and ran at the axeman behind me. His blade crashed through my shield from the top, sending a great chunk flying and chopping down to my forearm. The impact almost broke my arm but I threw my shield wide which yanked the axe from his hands and I smashed my blade into his face as I ran by him.

The edge of my blade was dented and bent by the earlier fighting. But even a blunt sword can smash a man's brains out if you swing it hard enough.

The next man, another Saracen, retreated from me, sensibly drawing toward the tunnel so that I would have my back to the other men.

But then Adelard was there. He cut down across the back of the Saracen. Then he impaled through the kidney the other man on that side of the cistern. The man jerked away, tearing Adelard's sword from his grasp. Adelard threw himself back from the mace that came at him. He ducked and dodged away.

Three of them left, not counting William.

I glanced over at William. He had his eyes closed and his head tilted back as if in prayer. The brazier fire blazed next to him so his face was flickering yellow and deep shadow. I had killed almost every one of his men and yet still William did not fight me.

There was movement a little way behind him against the far wall and for a moment I feared dozens of more men were waiting to attack. But then I saw that behind the fire was not the wall but a stockade. Arms stuck through upright wooden beams, joined by crosswise planks. Hands grasped. In the gaps between I saw faces.

It was full of people.

The people of the valley along with the survivors of William's raids.

Hugh of Havering came at me, with Roger of Tyre approaching and ready to fight with him. I felt the rage boil over and I hacked down into them one after the other, driving them down. I slipped in the blood and a sword point nicked my cheek.

I recovered but fell back. Blows rained onto my shield from both men. They moved with the same speed and ferocity as the Saracen and Hugo had upon the watchtower ruin. Their blows splintered my shield into tatters so I shook off the strap and flung it away

I blocked with my sword, trying to squirm and back off. It was hard to breathe and I was shaking. An unseen blow from Hugh or Roger got through and clanged against my helmet so hard I was sure my skull was caved in. But the good steel saved me and when my vision cleared I struck out with my foot and felt it connect with a knee or ankle. Roger fell and Hugh covered him until he got up and both backed away from the scything of my sword.

Adelard was retreating from the attack of the third man, a great bear of a fellow, and I staggered toward him.

William finally drew his sword. His face twisted in rage as he came for me. He positioned himself to cut me off from Adelard. My man got knocked from his feet, smashed down by a brutal blow from the bear knight. The bear knight raised up his mace for a blow that would crush Adelard's dazzled brain. The cistern was between me and Adelard. Hugh and Roger blocked one way around it. William walked forward, blocking the other.

In the centre of the room the dead woman spun on the

chain, suspended over the wide cistern of blood. I ran toward it, slipping but I jumped up, got a foot on the edge of the cistern and leapt for the woman. I grabbed her ankle with my shield hand. It was slippery with blood. I held on and swung myself over the cistern and landed with a crash against the man with the raised mace. We both fell. But I was on top. I got the edge of my blade across his throat and sawed back and forth, leaning into it with both hands and his blood frothed and spurted under the edge of the blade.

My breath rattled as I stood. Adelard hauled himself up beside me. We faced William and his two remaining men, Roger of Tyre and Hugh of Havering. The three of them standing together. But Adelard was puffing, exhausted and outclassed. I was at the limit of my endurance.

The three of them looked strong. They were fresh. I thought I understood why William had held himself back from the fighting. Around us came the groans of the dying.

"Why?" I asked William, hoping for a few moments with which to catch my breath. I looked at the lumpy, congealed blood in the cistern. It splashed underfoot across the floor. There were piles of fresh bodies against the far wall. The cistern held gallons of it. How many innocents had his men drained to make so much?

"At least tell me why this? What did these people do to you?"

"Why? Why, Richard? Blood is life," William sheathed his blade. He strode to the cistern, grabbed the edge. He plunged his face into that congealing mass. He gulped down mouthfuls and straightened again, swiping away lumpy strings of blood clots. William grinned a red smile.

"By this blood do I live. And by my blood my men gain a glimmer of my strength, my invulnerability. The Christ himself told us that unless you eat the flesh of the Christ and drink his blood, you do not have life within you. Whoever eats my body and drinks my blood remains in me and I in him. Are his words unclear, Richard?"

William slashed a tiny blade across the inside of his wrist and blood flowed and William offered out the wound. Hugh of Havering bent over and sunk his mouth onto the wound and drank it down, suckling the blood. I could hear the fevered gulping. He stopped and smacked his lips, grinning.

A smile spread across William's face. "And thus do we carry out God's divine will. What is the life of some peasant compared to taking this Blessed Sacrament?" Roger of Tyre bent to William's wrist and drank too.

"Sacrament?" I felt the rage returning. I glanced at the stockade beyond the fire where the prisoners were whimpering. "You are mad. And you have spread your madness to these other men." Bodies still writhed and groaned all across the floor. Men I had slain in pursuit of my personal justice.

"Madness?" William laughed, echoing from the walls. "Was it madness that brought me back from the dead at Hattin? Was it madness that made me drink the blood from the bodies piled upon me? It was a sign from God, there can be no doubt. I died but I was reborn."

I scoffed, even though I was almost convinced. "You were injured and you survived. The same has happened to me. Because of you, I died and they were going to bury me but I awoke and here I stand, ready to strike you down. I drank no blood to make it so. God gave you nothing. Your blood is not special."

William's smile faltered for a moment. He gestured to Hugh of Havering. "All men who take my Eucharist grow strong. If a man is injured a few drops heal his wounds. I take in the blood of women and children and within this holy vessel it is transformed into the blood of Christ. I do God's work."

"You killed my brother Henry because it was he who murdered your wife, I know that now. And if he truly did kill her? Then he deserved death."

William stared, unmoving. His men glanced at him and back to me.

"But you killed Alice. And you killed Isabella. And you

killed their children. And that was not God's work. It is for those crimes and for all the other innocent blood you have shed that I take my revenge."

"I killed them because they offended God," William said. "Why should Henry have happiness when he took mine? No, what I did to him was justice. What I did to our father was justice. I killed him for you, Richard. For you and for your mother."

I felt a terrible sinking feeling in my guts. "What is this madness that you speak now?"

William's mouth gaped. "You cannot mean that you do not know? You cannot be so dim witted if we are of the same blood? We are brothers, my dear Richard."

I shook my head, denying his words. Resisting the dawning realisation of their truth.

He grimaced. "Our father forced himself upon your mother, one Christmas if I recall. You are sprung from Robert de Ferrer's loins just as I am. Henry, that useless bastard you call brother, shared your mother but he despised you. You know that he hated you, surely? That hate was for what our father did to your mother. Did you know your mother slashed her wrists when you were a baby? Everyone pretended she had not but we all knew. Our father was the cause of it all." William's face twisted further into bitterness. "Perhaps it was that which drove Henry to kill my darling Katherine and my son Richard."

I felt the world turning under me once more. As hard as it was to believe, many things that had once seemed strange began to make sense.

The men in Dartmouth believed it was I that murdered the local girl. They thought I looked like William. I rarely saw my own reflection but I was of a height with him. We had the same dark hair, same build. And, I supposed, a similar face.

King Richard had said something about me inheriting some of the de Ferrers lands. *By rights it should be yours anyway.* My father's hatred for me. His attempts at making me a monk so that, even if Henry had died, I would never have inherited Ashbury. King Henry said that men were afraid I would be like William.

Such things only made sense if those kings had known or at least suspected the truth. How many men had known?

Had the Bishop of Coventry back in Derbyshire moved so quickly to take Duffield from fear that I would claim an inheritance and beat him to it? He gave me a full purse to encourage me to ride after William. But it was not to help me. I was delaying setting off and he must have wanted me to confront William. For even with a hired man or two I would have been killed had I found him.

I felt certain Alice had not known. Had not suspected.

Had she?

But William was still speaking.

"Henry never would have done such a thing if our father had not caused such violence to his mother. A violence that put a bastard in her belly. A violence that shamed her into self-murder. But I put things right. I did justice to all. I poisoned our father when I returned home. Poisoned him so thoroughly he was dead and cold in a single night." William laughed. It echoed from the walls. "But the old bastard woke up. Can you believe it? A day later, he lay on the table ready for burial and he sat up. He was very angry and I had to cut him down and bury him before the servants found out. It took rather a lot of work to kill him the second time. Practically had to cut his heart out. Tough old sod. We take after him, do we not? But know that he paid for his crime, though it was twenty years too late. I did it for you, Richard. Dearest Ricard, I take pride in telling you that your poor mother, God rest her soul, is avenged. As was my own mother, who died from the shame of her husband's ways. As was my wife, when I killed that evil little shit Henry of Ashbury."

I found I had little breath but William was looking at me. Waiting for me to speak.

"We are brothers," I managed to say.

William's eyes flashed sideways beyond me, changing

focus for the briefest of moments. His smile twitched.

A tiny movement in the corner of my eye.

"Adelard," I cried out, wheeling around.

But I was too late.

Antonius. The dark priest had crept after Adelard. He had freed himself from whatever bonds Adelard had left him in back in the tunnel. I watched as he rose up from behind us and sunk a dagger into Adelard's throat. He sawed it back and forth, blood welling out as Adelard screamed.

I smashed the priest's head so hard with my blade that his skull was almost cloven in two. Bone and pink brain sprayed out as I yanked back my sword.

William's men were on me. They were fast. I fell back under their assault, deflecting blows with my battered sword.

But I had tired. I was more exhausted than I had ever felt. I was hurting all over and both Hugh and Roger were full of renewed strength and speed. Where I had to block with the blade, their attacks jarred my sword arm hard.

There were bodies everywhere underfoot and they were hard to avoid.

I never even saw the sword that ran me through. The pain, though, was like fire and ice tearing through me. It had happened again. I was stabbed, run through the ribs.

My face was slapped, hard. I woke, knowing that it had been mere moments. Hugh and Roger held me by the shoulders suspended before William. The fire on the brazier felt hot and the metal sizzled.

"Does this feel familiar?" William asked. He was close.

I had failed.

"I told you this was God's will," William said, his breath reeking of blood.

"Yes," I said, a jolt of agony speared through me. "I see now."

William's face flowed before me. It was lit on one side by the fire that was finally dying now no one was there to feed it from the vast pile of desert brushwood. The wet blood on his face reflecting the flames like a thousand flecks of gold.

"So you see?" William asked. "You see I was given a gift by God?"

My head bobbed. "But I have it too," I said.

"No." William frowned. "You were not chosen," he said.

"We were born this way," I said. "Or perhaps we are born so and yet still we must die to become as we are. You killed me before but I was brought back. Just as you were at Hattin."

I coughed blood and darkness at the edges of my vision closed in.

William's face swam, a red and gold beacon in the darkness. "I have the Gift. I am the Angel of the Lord. I have the Christ's holy blood in my veins. Not you. Me."

"But Lord Robert, our father. You poisoned him and he died. But he, too, awoke."

"No!" He screamed in my face. "No, I was chosen, not you. Not father. Do you understand? Will you drink my blood and become my man or shall I drink you dry, brother?"

The stench of his breath made me gag and the convulsion wracked through me.

"Please, Lord," I mumbled. "Allow me to share your sacrament. Brother."

"You will serve me?" William asked. "Swear with God as your witness."

I was running out time and the world turned under me again. I saw then that oaths are worthless. Meaningless. Actions alone are important.

"I swear it,"

My eyes closed or I was losing consciousness. I heard but did not see William order his men to hold me steady. He warned them of my strength.

I felt skin pushed against my mouth. William intoned some twisted version of the ceremony as blood welled into my mouth.

My lips made a seal around his skin and I sucked in the hot blood that pumped and spurted into my mouth and swallowed it down. It was liquid gold. It was quicksilver. It was nectar and ambrosia.

In my travels I had felt the hunger of many days. I had felt the emptiness, weariness and weakness transformed after eating a piece of bread or meat. Felt the sustenance flow through my body and out into my limbs and into my mind, filling me up with strength once more.

Drinking William's blood was like filling up with lightning. It was wildfire in my heart. The hurricane in my lungs. The wound in my belly knitted together. My bones became iron. My muscles ached to be free, to throw down mountains and lay waste to cities.

Someone was growling. A low, threatening, evil cry that grew and rose to an animal cry like a wolf or a bear.

"What is happening?" I heard William cry. "Hold him, God damn you. Hold him still."

I stood. Neither man could resist my strength. I thrust my hands up and grabbed the throats of the two men beside me. Roger stabbed his dagger through my forearm up to the hilt but I felt nothing.

I crushed their throats to pulp, lifted them both from their feet by the neck and I tossed one after the other at William. He leapt aside from them both, their heads cracking on the floor and clattering against the piles of bodies in a loose-limbed jumble.

I stalked toward him. William snatched up a mace and swung it. It crunched into my arm and staggered me and he stepped in, sweeping it down on my head. I yanked it from him and swung it hard into his chest, ribs cracking like twigs. The force of the blow threw him back into the vast brazier. He thumped against it with his back and his head. It clanged and tossed up a shower of sparks.

"You are like me after all, brother," he said from under the brazier, eyes wild. "God has chosen us both." His voice pinched, his chest half crushed and struggling to breathe.

"No," I said, stalking forward, an animal growl coming from my chest.

"Come with me," William said, his eyes in shadow. "It is God's will that we be together."

"You will die by my hand," I said, stalking forward to finish him off. The strength his blood had provided was already dying away. Fading with every moment. But I had enough rage left to slaughter him a hundred times over.

He scowled. "We shall see," he said and he stood up, fast and heaved his back against the underside of the bowl of the brazier. He braced himself. William's back hissed as it pushed against the metal underside. He screamed and pushed harder, lifting it. Tilting it.

The brazier fell backward, the tripod legs lifting until finally it tipped and fell with a metallic crash. It flung the contents of the bowl into the stockade and against the huge pile of brushwood. Half a hundredweight of glowing charcoal and flame tossed into a tinderbox.

Screams came from inside the stockade as the straw underfoot ignited and spread. I watched, mouth agape, at the speed with which the ancient timbers sparked into flame.

I turned back for William. To finish him. But already he was up and scuttling round behind me, back to the blood cistern in the centre of the room. His chest was smashed and he bent double. Yet he grinned and ducked his head into the cistern, gulping down more of the glistening, thick liquid.

The Saracens in the stockade screamed and rattled the wooden bars. They were shut in behind a sturdy door that was already on fire. The wooden beams that kept them in were too thick for them to break.

William backed away from me, snatching up a sword. "Fight me and they burn. All those women and children." He stood straight again. His voice was strong and his breathing steady.

"I will kill you," I said but made no move toward him.

"You forget I know you like a brother." He laughed,

pointing at the fire. At the stockade. "Your wife's children are within."

William turned and strode away toward the tunnel, his laughter echoing from the walls of the cavern as he disappeared into the darkness.

I ignored his escape, scooped up a huge axe and ran to the wall of flame. Between the bars, I could see the movement of the people screaming in terror. Flame leapt and crackled along the floor. The straw underfoot had caught and none of their frantic stamping helped to stem the blaze.

The huge axe was a whirlwind as I chopped through the beams farthest from the flames. Chips of wood flew. Flames crept closer until I was hacking into burning wood and the heat singed my hair and scolded my skin. I was sure I was too late, too weak, too slow but then the wood cracked and I kicked it through.

Hands and arms appeared and I pulled them through. I yanked out one after the other while the fire spread and the smoke choked us. Women and children, mostly. My eyes filled with smoke. The flames grew until the fire engulfed the hole and the people I dragged through were burned.

I used my body to shield them as best I could. I pushed my back against the flames until they were all through. The pain lashed me, spasms wracked my body. My helmet and armour were roasting me alive.

I had not seen Alice's children. William had lied to me. Romantic fool that I was I had allowed myself to be tricked. William did know me. And yet for all that I was burning, I forced my head through the gap and squinted through the pain and the choking fumes.

Shapes moved in the corner against the back wall. I clambered through. Two children clasping each other.

Jocelyn and little Emma.

I was passing out from the smoke and burns on my skin so I grabbed the children, kicked out more of the burning wood and hurled them through the gap.

On the other side I carried them away to the other side of the cavern where it was lit by a tiny lamp.

My seared skin cracked and oozed as I set the children down beyond the blood. Black smoke billowed in a layer above our heads, getting thicker and lower. The other prisoners were panicking at the far end of the cavern, shrieking and wailing, trying to get out. It was dark and they could not find the entranceway.

Jocelyn clung to my arm, his strong fingers digging into my burned skin.

Emma was not moving.

My hands and eyes were shaking and I could not tell whether she was breathing. If only I had some of William's blood.

William's blood.

I seized my dagger, stabbed my wrist and held it over Emma's mouth. Blood dropped onto her lips.

"No," Jocelyn wailed. "Do not make her one of them."

"She will not be," I said, my voice a raw whisper from the smoke. "And if I do not, she may die."

He nodded once, giving me permission. His trust moved me deeply. It was not merely the smoke that made my eyes run with tears.

I worried about drowning Emma with my blood but still I held my wrist to her mouth. Her lips stirred and her throat bobbed. Her eyes sprang open. She gulped down life and her fingers dug into my arm like claws. When her eyes were alight with astonishment I gave her to her brother, who held her to his strong little body. She had recovered enough to walk and I knew she would live.

But I was dying. I could feel black poison from the burns seeping into my flesh. I knew what I needed.

The vat of blood had been warmed by the fire. I climbed up and in and submerged myself, the thick substance covering my head and I lapped it up, drinking down that filth, that life. Gulping down chunks of clotted blood, I came up for air, vomited black blood and drank more until my belly was bulging.

And the strength of it flowed through me. My burns were soothed and my skin became whole and soft again.

I climbed out, blood slewing off of my helm, my hauberk in sheets. The prisoners gathered, stood staring at me in fear, pleading for help. They were coughing, suffocating and terrified of the blood-drenched Frankish knight before them. Poor souls lost in the darkness and had come back to the light of the raging flame, looking to me to help them once again.

Carrying Jocelyn and Emma in my arms, I lead the peasants out through the tunnel. I groped my way through darkness and smoke until a prick of light appeared ahead. I staggered up from the black hole gasping for air and life.

Dawn was breaking over the hills. It was astonishing that I had been underground for so little time. A pale pink light growing and the promised warmth of the day already in the wind. Smoke drifted from holes all over the hill until the underground blaze burnt itself out. I looked from every vantage and not a soul moved anywhere down in the valleys or across the hills. From somewhere, a single goat bleated.

William was long gone.

The local Saracens helped each other away down into the valley. Those folk I had saved kept as far away from me as possible. Many glanced back at me, their faces masks of despair.

I found and collected our horses and fed the children with what food and water remained in the packs.

We rode for Acre.

∞

"So dozens of men and women died but you let William escape," Henry of Champagne, King of Jerusalem said to me, some months later in Acre. "In fact, everyone died but you and William, is that correct?"

It was not correct but I was in no mood for rising to his bait and I said nothing. It was another informal audience in the cool room at the top of his palace. Such was the desire to keep my actions as quiet as possible. I stood before him while he lounged ungraciously with the Archbishop sat next to him.

"Richard is to be congratulated," the Archbishop said, smiling and inviting the king to share in his praise of me. "He put an end to William's raids and trade is now flowing once again. He stopped the abductions of the locals and returned many innocents to their homes. Surely Saladin will be grateful to you for the fact it was a Frank that saved them."

"I doubt that," Henry said and drank more of his wine. "And William is free to start again at any moment."

"Not in your kingdom, sire," I said. "He fled north, I am certain of it. Near Tiberius two weeks later there was a woman with her throat savaged. A few weeks after that I heard of two children wounded about the neck at Antioch. They were buried by the time I arrived but I am certain it was William. There were other tales that may have been him but his trail went cold not far into Anatolia. I was most unwelcome there, as you might expect. Then I spoke to merchants who told me of more sudden deaths in Antioch so I returned, thinking William had also doubled back on me. But it was just a bloody flux and I could find no further trace of him."

"So, you failed," the King of Jerusalem said. "I think that perhaps it is convenient that William walks away from this unharmed. I do not say that you were in collusion with the man but this is all too convenient, too convenient by far."

I was thinking that it was convenient for the king that his guards had taken my sword at the palace gates. But still I imagined dragging him from his chair and beating him senseless. Perhaps the Archbishop could read my thoughts.

"William is gone from your kingdom, sire," the Archbishop said, quickly. "Certainly gone and likely gone for good. And if ever he dares show his face once more, then Richard will most certainly slay him, will you not, Richard?"

"William shall die by my sword," I said, picturing that

very thing.

The king looked like he had a bad taste in his mouth. "I suppose I must present you with land and a title," he said. "As a reward for scouring out and destroying William's raiding camp and preserving our fragile peace. It is good land, I stayed there once, I think. It will bring you a better income than that accursed pile of dirt outside Jaffa. Income to buy men and men's tales of William. Your search will go better with it, will it not?"

And, of course, he wanted me as an ally to help protect his fragile kingdom. There was no denying now that I was a great knight.

"I am grateful, my lord," I said.

I shall not live, I shall not die until William lies dead by my sword. I would take the land but if Henry called upon me to fight I would have to deny him. William would have to come first. But not because of any oath. My duty was to the dead.

"Good, then. Speak to my chamberlain, he will see to everything. Now, go. Go and find a wife and when the Saracens stir themselves again, you shall help me win the war."

I took my leave from the king, my liege lord, and he waved me away while sinking another cup of wine.

The Archbishop rose and accompanied me out of the

room and into the corridor where he placed a hand upon my arm. He still gripped his cup of wine in his other gnarled hand.

"You are deeply troubled, Richard," he said as the door was closed behind us.

"William lives," I said.

The Archbishop sighed and sat upon the bench that ran along the wall. "Sit," he said and patted the bench next to his backside. "My old bones ache. I find I need rest more often every month. Every day, some times. It shall not be long before I finally join God in Heaven." He leaned over to me and lowered his voice conspiratorially. "I find that wine, the very best wine, you understand, is the one thing that helps with the pain."

I sat. It was quiet. Through the door to the king's chamber I could hear muffled voices as the king's men got on with the business of governing and the king got on with drinking. I was burdened by what I knew and I wanted the old man to believe me. But how could I convince him?

"What of the children?" the Archbishop asked, softly.

"The boy Jocelyn and his sister I took to Alice's mother's sister in Jaffa," I said.

"Do you have no love for the children?" He asked it softly but it was a cruel question and he twisted it further into my guts. "You are now the lone other soul in the world who they know. Can you truly abandon them to distant relatives?"

"Leaving them with a family they do not know may be the greatest sin I have committed, my lord Archbishop," I said. "I am aware of the agony those children are in. But leave them I must. With William roaming free, my presence may bring death down upon them once more."

And seeing them reminded me of Alice.

"Who better to protect them?" he asked.

"I tell you I am dangerous," I said.

I would confuse them and upset them if I went to see them, I told myself. It was cowardice, of course. I could not face the loss of my wife. Thinking of those children made me think of her. When I thought of her I felt like dying. The horror of it was that her death was my own fault. I had fought to become a knight worthy of her but I had thought that meant having wealth and social standing. If she had never met me, if she had rejected me, then she would have been alive to be mother to those children. The only way I could cope with such thoughts was to pretend I did not have them.

"And how are they, Richard?" he asked, again, gently.

"Jocelyn is angry at everything," I said. "When he is older he will come into some of his father's land in Poitou. He is seven, now, I think. I told him to train hard and to become a good knight before then and if he ever needed my help I would fight alongside him. He's a good lad. The girl, Emma. She does not speak. Perhaps, in time. She is yet very young and has time to mend."

"Well, quite," the Archbishop said, nodding. "I shall pray for them."

"Would you look in on them, my lord?" I asked, my throat tight. "From time to time?" It was an absurd request for he was just a couple of steps down from God Himself.

"I shall keep an eye on them," the Archbishop said. "I suppose I owe them that much, for my part."

I thanked him sincerely.

"I shall pray for you too, Richard. I shall pray for your soul."

"Pray for William's soul," I said, ungratefully. "For he shall be facing judgement soon enough."

Such words come as easily as breathing. But words mean nothing and the Archbishop knew I was full of bile and nonsense.

"I do pray for William's soul," he said. "Anger and bitterness, if he holds on to such things, fill up a man's soul until there is nothing left that is good and decent." He peered up at me.

"I do not wish to be like William," I said, irritated. "Perhaps it truly was the death of his wife and son that turned him so completely to evil. It is likely that it sent him mad. But he was vindictive and cruel from birth."

The Archbishop nodded. "I see now what is troubling you."

"My wife is dead. Her death was my doing and I have failed even to bring justice to her murderer. It is years now since I swore an oath, to Isabella, to slay William and every day is another day of failure. Of course I am troubled. My lord."

"You have slain all of Williams's followers. Six of whom were the vilest, deadliest creatures who walked or crawled upon the earth. You have scoured him from the Holy Land. If I were you I should call such victories a success." The Archbishop shifted his buttocks on the hard bench. "But you fear that you are as William is, do you not?"

"Does every man in Christendom know that he and I are brothers?" The shame of my ignorance made my face burn.

I felt him shrug beside me, his robes rustling softly. "Perhaps only to those few of us who have known you both. You are so very similar to each other. In stature and features. Your manner of speech is almost identical. It would not be the first time an overlord has forced himself upon his vassal's wife. I am sorry to hear that the old Earl died unpunished."

"William returned to Derbyshire to kill his father. Our father."

"Good God."

I found I had a burning need to tell the Archbishop everything. "William said he killed our father with poison. Earl Robert was dead and cold but then he woke up and William had to kill him again."

"Terrible. A terrible sin."

"Do you not see, my lord?" I said. "Does the tale not sound familiar to you? William was cut down and tossed into a pile of corpses at Hattin. He was truly dead. Do you think the Saracens are so incompetent that they cannot ensure we are dead? They stab us before they strip our bodies. William died. Then he was reborn and reborn fully healed with strength enough to fight his way clear. Perhaps he truly did kill forty Saracens in his escape."

"Once I thought it was a miracle. Now I doubt it happened at all."

"I tell you it may well be the truth. I know that when I was reborn I found myself with greater strength that I ever had before."

He looked up at me. "When you were reborn."

"William's men killed me. At my estate, when Alice was killed, I was stabbed many times, deeply, in the chest."

"Your robustness is well known, Richard."

"I was always remarkably quick to heal, yes. Which in itself is very strange, is it not? But these wounds were different. I have seen more men killed than I can count and I know for certain that no man could have suffered so and lived."

"And yet you did. A flaw in your reasoning."

"I died. My servants said I was cold and lifeless for a day before I woke up. And when I did, I found that I was stronger, faster. And a good thing, too, because William's men possessed their master's own strength."

"William's men were the risen dead, also? Come, Richard, you go too far. You were out in the hills too long."

"They were not dead but had drunk William's blood. His blood has power. Power to heal wounds. Power to grant strength and speed."

He looked gravely concerned. "I am beginning to fear you have become as mad as William."

"There is more," I said. "My own blood holds the same power."

"Because you are brothers?"

"We were both grown from our father's seed. Why would it not? When I pulled the children from the smoke, Emma was dying. I gave her a few drops of my blood and she woke. Fully healed and full of life."

"Are you saying you imbued her with the strength of a

knight?"

I smiled at the thought. "The strength of a strong girl, perhaps. The powers last no longer than a week, and they fade over that time. Emma is returned to her old self."

"I must say, I struggle to believe what you are telling me. You have always seemed a sober, reasoned young man."

I plucked the cup from his hands, stood and tossed the wine from the window.

"That was a particularly fine Burgundy."

I took my dagger and pierced my thumb where the large vein is and squeezed my blood into his cup.

"If you think I am going to drink that then you truly have lost your mind," the Archbishop said.

"My mind is perfectly clear," I said, taking my seat by him again while my blood spurted into the cup. "It has grown clearer and stronger ever since I died. Whatever it was that happened to me, the change in me was for the better. My whole life I was amongst the fastest and strongest. But since I woke from death it is as though all other normal men are wading through mud." There was enough blood in the cup for a mouthful. I pinched my thumb, stopping the flow. The smell of it was strong and good and it glistened, dark and shiny in the shadow of the cup. I looked at the Archbishop, seeing disgust and wariness in his eyes. But also curiosity. He wanted to believe me.

"If you taste this," I said. "I am certain that the aches in your bones will ease. For no more than a week or so but you might feel young again."

"What makes you think I want to feel young again? I am perfectly happy being old. God wills it. And the only blood I will drink is the blood of the Christ. This smacks of blasphemy."

His protestations were so weak that I was sure he needed no more than a nudge.

"I swear it is true and if it does not work then I shall do whatever penance you instruct of me."

He paused and I knew I had him.

"Richard, I would not make a man do penance for madness. I may have you thrown into a dungeon until you stop this raving."

"Here," I said and gave him the cup.

"God forgive me," he said. He looked down the corridor to be sure no other man was there and drank, grimacing. Good on the old man; he knocked it right back and handed me the cup.

"How do you feel?" I asked as he wiped his mouth.

"I must say that was the vilest—" he froze. His eyes widened until I could see the whites all around and his pupils grew until they were enormous black pits. He sprang to his feet, knocking the wine cup clattering into the corner.

He bent his knees, bouncing up and down. The Archbishop stretched his hands up above his head and then squeezed his knees and shoulders and he laughed.

"The pain is gone," he said, his voice breathy and excited. "I feel as though I could leap from this window and fly."

I laughed. "Please do not try that."

"You feel like this all the time?" he said, flexing his hands and peering at the knuckles.

"Perhaps even more so," I said. "William gave his blood to his men and they became more than they were. But still I was quicker than they were. Mostly. But when I tasted William's blood myself it was as though the power was many times stronger still. I remember William's astonishment at the ease with which I killed his men. My body could scarcely contain it. Thankfully, it lasted but a few moments."

"By God," he said, full of wonder. "I am sorry I ever doubted you."

The chamber door opened beside us and one of the king's men came bustling out carrying a bundle of scrolls, begged our pardon and walked by.

"Let us take some air, Richard," the Archbishop said and before I could reply he had hitched up his robes and charged off toward the stairs. He barged the king's attendant out of the way, sending scrolls bouncing all over the place. I heard him laughing as he ran.

Following the trail of startled servants, I caught up with the Archbishop in the palace gardens. He had his legs planted wide, hands on his hips looking up at the sky. It was a cool day but the air was crisp and clear.

"You have a gift, Richard," he said as I drew near to him.

"I wonder," I said. "Perhaps it is a curse? For William and I are the same. And William is evil."

The Archbishop turned to me and his face was full of joy. "I do not believe that this could be an evil thing."

"And yet," I said. "If William and I drink human blood, we become even stronger than we are." I explained what had happened in the cavern. My burns and how I healed them.

He shook his head in wonder. "God is so very mysterious."

"You asked how I could abandon the children," I said. "The truth is that I wonder if I am a danger to them."

"But you would not harm children, Richard. You saved them. You are a good man."

I said nothing.

"Perhaps William is cursed," the Archbishop said. "But perhaps God has given you this gift so that you may stop him. So that you may be a perfect counter to his evil."

"I am not that good, Archbishop," I said. "His evil knows no bounds and I myself am full of sin."

"Then be as good as you can," he said. "We are all sinners but it was you who was given this gift. Whatever God's reasons take comfort in knowing that he has a plan for you."

I suppose I felt comforted. I thanked him.

"You say this shall last less than one week?" he asked.

"It will fade until you are just as you were before," I said.

"Do you know," the Archbishop said. "I have not run like I just did since... I do not know that I ever ran before in all my life. Even when I was a boy. Do you know what else I have never done? Swam in the sea. Care to join me?"

In those days no one swam. I laughed. "They will call us madmen," I said, grinning. "And I do not know how."

"I am the Archbishop and soon I shall be dead. I care only what God thinks of me. And we shall learn how. Come on, you coward. Race you there."

He lived almost two more years. The last time I saw him he was wasted away into nothing, laying in his bed. I offered him more blood and I saw he was tempted but he refused. I mourned him.

After I had climbed from that cavern of blood, I stayed in Outremer, Cyprus and the lands of Byzantium for seven more years. Always I was moving from place to place, living in cities for months or even years, listening for tales of blood. God knows, there enough of those but none led to

William.

King Henry of Jerusalem died, tumbling from a window like an idiot. There were whispers of assassination but drunks often come to foolish ends. The new king, my liege lord, did not know me and was irritated by my existence. A steady stream of knights and other madmen arrived in Outremer, my few acquaintances died or returned to Europe and I saw new faces everywhere.

I was tired. Tired of the Holy Land. Tired of hiding from the world and of watching it go by without having any real part of it or having any significant connection with anyone. Tired of loneliness. I had grown sick of the heat, of the dust and the memories but still I waited for William to show himself again. Certainly, he could not have gone to any of the vast Plantagenet lands for King Richard would have had him arrested.

Then, in the summer of 1199, news reached Acre that Richard the Lionheart was dead.

The greatest soldier of the age had been killed by a child shooting a crossbow bolt into his neck in a petty squabble in Poitou. Richard had survived countless battles since childhood and recovered from many terrible illnesses and still no man could equal his vitality. Perhaps that was why he stood before the walls of that worthless castle with no armour. Then a boy, orphaned in the conflict, chanced a lucky shot. The boy was brought before the king. Richard commanded that the terrified lad be awarded a hundred shillings for dutifully protecting his lord and avenging his father. That part had enough of Richard's saintly bravado about it for me to believe it. It was a shame, then, that as soon as the king died the boy was flayed alive.

Of course, Richard's death presented an opportunity for William. Without the Lionheart's fury directed against him, William could make a case to the crown to be reinstated lord of the de Ferrers lands.

So I returned to England. It was my yearning for a home more than my duty to the dead. But I convinced myself that William would be unable to resist the lure of his Earldom.

I was half right.

William was being worshipped as a Green Knight and lord of Eden by a band of outlaws deep in the ancient forest of Sherwood near Nottingham. He was in disguise, using his father's name Robert. And he was going about cloaked and hooded, robbing coin and drinking blood from rich and poor alike.

But that is a tale for another time.

AUTHOR'S NOTE

Richard's story continues in Vampire Outlaw the Immortal Knight Chronicles Book 2. Out now.

If you enjoyed Vampire Crusader please leave a review! Even a couple of lines saying what you like about the story would be an enormous help and mean the book is more visible to new readers.

You can find out more and get in touch with me at dandavisauthor.com

BOOKS BY DAN DAVIS

The GALACTIC ARENA Series

Science fiction

Inhuman Contact
Onca's Duty
Orb Station Zero

The IMMORTAL KNIGHT Chronicles

Historical Fiction - with Vampires

Vampire Crusader
Vampire Outlaw

GUNPOWDER & ALCHEMY

Flintlock Fantasy

White Wind Rising
Dark Water Breaking
Green Earth Shaking

For a complete and up-to-date list of Dan's available books,
visit: **http://dandavisauthor.com/books/**